# THE UNLUCKY PRINCE

**Once Upon A Prince**

The Unlucky Prince by Deborah Grace White
The Beggar Prince by Kate Stradling
The Golden Prince by Alice Ivinya
The Wicked Prince by Celeste Baxendell
The Midnight Prince by Angie Grigaliunas
The Poisoned Prince by Kristin J. Dawson
The Silver Prince by Lyndsey Hall
The Shoeless Prince by Jacque Stevens
The Silent Prince by C. J. Brightley
The Crownless Prince by Selina R. Gonzalez
The Awakened Prince by Alora Carter
The Winter Prince by Constance Lopez
***Grab the whole Once Upon A Prince series today!***

# DEBORAH GRACE WHITE

# THE UNLUCKY PRINCE

ONCE UPON A PRINCE

A FROG PRINCE RETELLING

*For Reuben*
*Keep focusing on the details that are important to you as you find*
*your own adventure.*

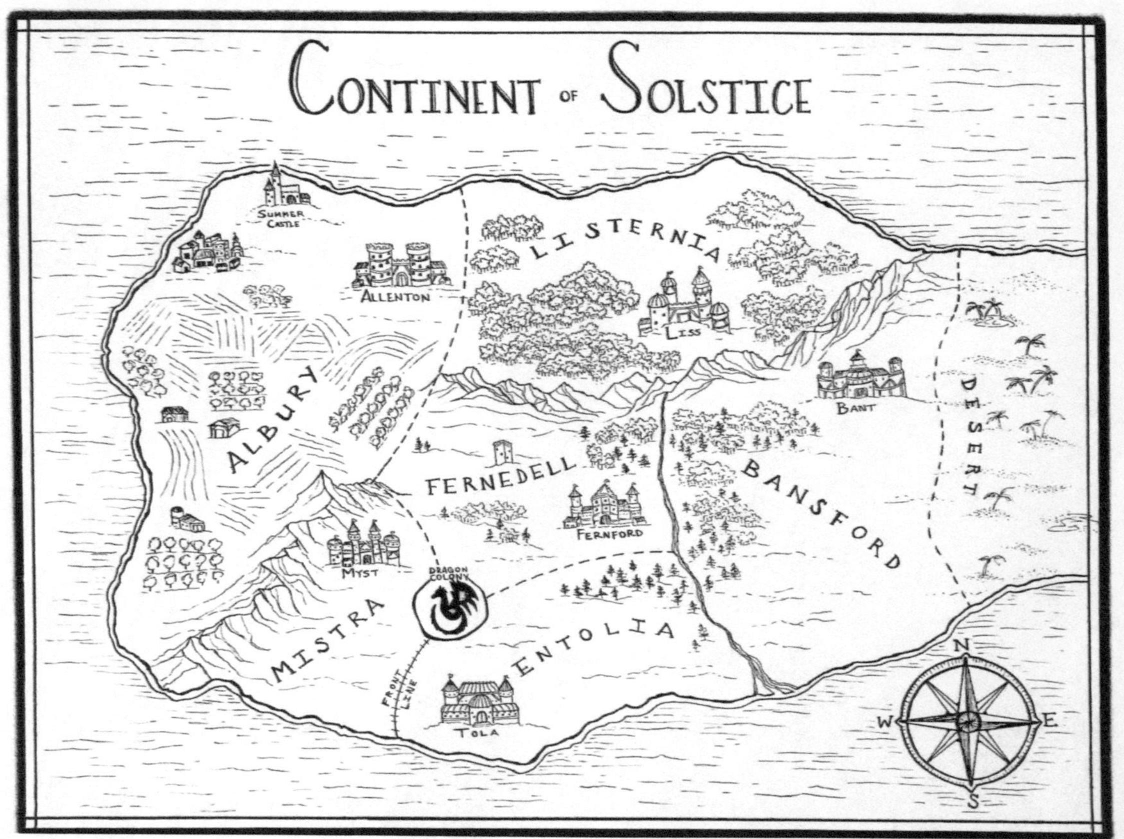

Continent of Solstice
Summer Castle
Allenton
LISTERNIA
Liss
Bant
DESERT
ALBURY
FERNEDELL
Fernford
BANSFORD
Myst
Dragon Colony
MISTRA
ENTOLIA
Front Line
Tola
N
E
S
W

Royal family of Entolia

Dowager Queen Lucille
- King Basil (23), married to Queen Wren (22)
  - Prince Teddy (3)
  - Princess Azure (1.5)
- Princess Zinnia (22), married to Obsidian (25)
  - Genevieve/Genny (2)
- Princess Lilac (21)
- Princess Violet (19)
- Princess Daisy (17)
- Princess Briar (16)
- Princess Jasmine (14)
- Princess Magnolia (14)
- Princess Cassia (12)
- Princess Dahlia (11)
- Princess Holly (9)
- Princess Ivy (9)
- Princess Wisteria (8)

# CHAPTER ONE

## Ari

"How much further to the border?" Ari pushed up in the saddle, trying to see over the slight rise ahead. Once they left his own kingdom of Mistra and crossed into Entolia, they would be less than a day's ride from Tola, Entolia's capital city and their current destination.

"We're almost there, Your Highness," said his nearest companion calmly, looking like he was trying not to smile at the prince's enthusiasm.

Showing no such restraint, Ari grinned broadly at the grizzled senior servant. "You probably think I'm foolish to be excited about this journey, don't you, Lex? You think it'll all come to nothing."

The older man shrugged, a smile tugging up one corner of his lips. He'd been serving Mistra's royal family since well before Ari was born, so he could have gotten away with speaking his mind, but he didn't take the liberty.

It was another man who spoke, drawing his horse up on Ari's other side.

"It may well come to nothing. I think Your Highness should

prepare yourself for the possibility that the rumors regarding an expedition across the desert are simply that—rumors."

Ari held in a scowl at Lord Golding's dampening words. He hadn't asked for the nobleman's opinion. He hadn't asked for his presence, either. But he knew he shouldn't complain. The inclusion of a lone diplomatic representative from his father's court was more of a concession than he'd expected when he pleaded with his parents to let him travel without a formal delegation.

"You sound like my mother, Lord Golding," he said, speaking lightly. He turned to Lex again. "Oh, that reminds me, I meant to extend my particular thanks to you, Lex, after my mother spoke to me as we were leaving Myst the other day." He named the capital of his own kingdom, Mistra.

The servant looked surprised. "What did Her Majesty say, Your Highness?"

Ari shrugged. "Oh, the usual. That no good will come of me indulging my restlessness, and I'd do much better to settle down and get married like my brothers have all done, rather than gallivanting off across the continent looking for adventure." He sighed. "I'm not trying to be difficult, you know. I wish I could have adjusted back to *normal* life as smoothly as my brothers have, but to be honest, I still feel like a stranger in my own body sometimes."

This speech was met with silence from both of his companions. Although they looked equally uncomfortable, only Lex was visibly bewildered. Ari walked himself back through their conversation and realized his error.

He laughed. "Oh, sorry, you meant what did she say about you that made me want to thank you, didn't you? Well, she told me that you specifically volunteered to accompany me. And I wanted to let you know that I appreciate it." He grinned again. "Especially given that you no doubt think the whole journey is a wild goose chase, even if you're too polite to say so."

He leaned up in his saddle again, peering ahead before looking back at the servant.

Lex relaxed, although his expression was a little hard to read as he glanced over at Ari. "I don't think your excitement about a journey is unnatural, Your Highness," he said. "But I will acknowledge that I don't share your enthusiasm to reach the front lines."

"Former front lines," Ari corrected him, frowning at this way of describing the border between Mistra and the neighboring kingdom of Entolia. "The war with Entolia has been over for five years, Lex. It's just a border now."

"Yes, Your Highness," said the servant, something about his tone telling Ari that he wasn't convinced.

The prince eyed the older man thoughtfully. He hadn't put his finger on it, but now he was taking note, he realized that Lex had seemed to grow a little stiffer the closer they got to the border. "Did you visit the front lines during the years of the war?" he asked. "I'd thought you always lived in the capital."

The servant cleared his throat. "I was stationed there twice," he said. "Not as a soldier, but as part of my royal duties, during periods where frequent visits were necessary from the castle. Each appointment lasted a few months."

"I didn't know that," Ari said, chastened. "I'm sorry if this trip is bringing back bad memories." He looked ahead, finally catching sight of a neat cluster of buildings. "But it's nothing like it was then," he assured his companion. "And I know, because I saw it during the war as well." He chuckled. "Although it looked a little different from a bird's eye view."

Neither Lord Golding nor Lex showed any sign of humor at his joke. On the contrary, both men shifted in their saddles, and Ari sighed. He was used to the reaction—many people in Myst were still absurdly uncomfortable at any mention of the curse that had caused him and his five older brothers to spend six years trapped in the bodies of swans. Honestly, the awkwardness was a big part of why he'd found it hard to settle back into regular life. If he was allowed to talk about his experiences freely, he probably wouldn't feel so unsettled.

Their passage across the border was uneventful. It did indeed look different from the battleground it had once been, when Mistra and Entolia had been mired in a six-year long conflict over their border. Ari had actually crossed it once since then, when he'd attended his sister's wedding four years previously. Wren, Mistra's sole princess, had married King Basil of Entolia. It was still strange for Ari to think that Wren was his graceless little sister no longer—she was the queen of a foreign kingdom, and very poised these days.

They'd broken camp early that morning, at Ari's request, in the hope that they'd make Tola in time for dinner. He wasn't disappointed. The sun was only just on the point of setting when they crested a rise and the Entolian capital came into view.

The city of Tola was perched along a shoreline which went from sandy cove to rugged cliff over the length of the city. The castle sat at the city's eastern edge, atop the cliffs. It was hard to get a good look at it in the waning light, but Ari remembered it from his previous visit. It wasn't much like the grand castle in which he'd grown up. It was pleasant enough, but not what he'd call elaborate. He'd heard it described as overlooking the city from the cliffs, and before his first visit, he'd imagined an imposing facade rising above the lesser dwellings, like the jewel on the crown that was Entolia's capital.

The first time he'd seen it for himself, however, Tola's castle had reminded Ari more of a tolerant uncle watching over his family benignly. It was long and low, running parallel to the ocean, and even the stone dragons that flanked the entrance looked more comfortable than intimidating.

The group was expected, but no great fanfare met their arrival. Ari thought Lord Golding looked irked. But personally he was delighted to be received not by any stuffy display, but by his sister hurrying toward him with her daughter on her hip and a beaming smile on her face.

"Ari! You made it!"

"Wren." Ari embraced his sister, pausing to tweak the dark ringlets clustered around his little niece's face. "Azure has so much hair now!"

"I know," Wren said, smiling fondly at her daughter. "She's a year and a half, can you believe it? A whole year since we were last in Myst."

She turned to the other members of Ari's small party, greeting them with gentle courtesy. "I'm sorry Basil can't be here to receive you all," she said. "He's in a meeting he couldn't slip away from, but he'll join us for dinner shortly."

"Oh, no need for him to rush away on my account," said Ari cheerfully. "King duties trump visits from the least of his brothers-in-law."

"Nonsense, he'll be delighted you're here. And," she informed him sternly, "youngest does not mean least."

Ari nudged her shoulder. "You should know, pipsqueak."

He thought the ladies' maid attending Wren looked a little scandalized at this form of addressing the queen, but Wren just chuckled.

"Rooms have been prepared for all of you, of course. You have a little time to freshen up. I'll see you at dinner." She gave him another hug, providing the perfect opportunity for little Azure to grab his ear and tug vigorously.

"Zuzu!" Wren scolded her daughter, gently removing the offending hand. She grimaced at her brother. "Sorry."

"It's all right," Ari laughed, tweaking his niece's hair again. The toddler graced him with an enormous grin. "She's going to be trouble, this one," he commented.

Wren gave him a long-suffering look. "She already is," she assured him. "See you at dinner."

Still chuckling, Ari followed a servant to a lavish guest suite on the far side of the castle. He didn't spend long there, however. Reaching his destination at last had given him new energy. He only planned to stay in Tola for a week before continuing eastward, and he was eager not to waste a minute of it. He'd met the Entolian royals when he came for Wren and Basil's wedding, but that had been four years ago, and the visit had been mainly taken up with formalities. He'd made no real connection with any of them, and he felt the need to re-introduce himself. Wren described family life in the Entolian castle as *chaos, but the endearing kind*, and he was looking forward to experiencing it.

When he entered the dining hall where the royal family ate, however, he immediately realized that he hadn't sufficiently prepared himself for the chaos. King Basil's father had died years previously, but his mother was there, seated at one end of a long table, looking impressively serene given her surroundings. Everyone else at the spread was from Ari's generation or younger. And there were a lot of them.

Growing up with five older brothers and a little sister, Ari had always thought of his family as large. But the family Wren had married into put them to shame. Basil had no brothers, but he had twelve younger sisters, all of whom seemed to be present. As far as Ari knew, only one of those sisters was married—Princess Zinnia, who had created a bit of a stir when she married an untitled soldier. Although he was an enchanter, and the ability to use magic was rare enough that it gave him clout similar to a nobleman's title.

The pair in question were seated at the far end of the table, Princess Zinnia chatting animatedly with another sister, while Obsidian spoke softly to the small child on his knee, presumably their daughter.

That was another surprise. When he'd been shown to the family's smaller dining hall, Ari had realized it wasn't to be a formal state reception, and he'd been glad of it. But he hadn't expected the children to actually be present. In addition to the child on Obsidian's knee, he could see Azure sitting on Wren's lap, and Wren's three-year-old son Teddy bouncing on his own seat alongside his mother.

On reflection, Ari could imagine how foolish it would seem for anyone to forbid the attendance of the little children when the youngest of King Basil's sisters—theoretically in the same generation as the king and queen, and Ari himself—was only eight years old. The younger of the princesses were certainly giving their infant nieces and nephew fair competition in both volume and energy. And yet, no one seemed troubled by the general cacophony, even the dowager queen seeming unruffled.

Ari hovered uncertainly by the door for a moment, before Wren caught sight of him and waved him over.

"There's a seat here for you, Ari," she told him in her quiet way when he was close enough to hear. After directing him to a seat across from her, she cast a look around the group, as though she intended to properly introduce him, then seemed to give up on the idea of getting all their attention.

At that moment, the door swung open again, saving her the necessity. All conversation paused as King Basil strode into the room with swift steps.

"Sorry to keep you all waiting," he told his family cheerfully. He moved straight to the place beside his wife, stooping to kiss her cheek before swooping his son up into his arms. "Over you go, Teddy," he said, his voice perfectly pleasant as he supplanted the child to the next seat over, allowing the young king to sit beside his wife. The moment King Basil was seated, the three-year-old rebelled against his orders, clambering up onto his father's lap, where he was received with a loose arm around his shoulders.

The arrival of the king was obviously the servants' cue, because they started to lay dishes on the table at once. Basil's eyes met Ari's across the spread, and his face lit in a smile of welcome.

"Ari! I forgot you were arriving this evening, my apologies for not greeting you properly." He cleared his throat, and instantly had everyone's attention. "Everyone, you remember the youngest of Wren's older brothers, Ari. We're delighted to have him with us."

Every eye turned to Ari, a dozen friendly greetings tumbling over one another. He smiled, waving a hand in recognition, and marveling at how informal they were all allowed to be. It was a far cry from life in his own castle.

"Are you one of the ones who used to be a swan?" demanded one of the younger princesses. If she was as old as ten, Ari would be surprised.

"Ivy," said the dowager queen, exasperated, but Ari was grinning.

"Yes, but that doesn't make me special, you know. We all were swans, except for Wren. So it doesn't set me apart in the least."

"We all know that feeling," joked the princess seated next to Ari. He turned to her, expecting to see another child, and was surprised to find a young woman.

"It's still remarkable to us, though," chimed in another sister, this one a teenager. "What was it like? How could you retain your human mind while in a bird's body? Did you still have your normal thoughts, or was your mind consumed by…I don't know, hunting for worms?"

"I had my own thoughts," Ari assured her solemnly. "I can't speak to how intelligent they were, but that issue predated being turned into a swan." The young woman beside him chuckled, and he allowed himself a grin. "And it was a very bad day if I had to survive off worms."

"Ick!" said one of the younger girls, a few of them giggling over the thought of eating worms. The teenage one looked like she was gearing up for another question, but her mother cut her off.

"Enough, Briar. Let's not interrogate Prince Ari with questions about the affliction he suffered."

"I don't mind, Your Majesty," Ari said, smiling politely at the dowager queen.

"Good of you," Basil cut in, "but we'll let you enjoy the status of guest for at least one evening before we start grilling you with questions at every meal."

He deftly turned the conversation, and Ari directed his attention to the food in front of him. The king probably thought he was shielding his brother-in-law, but Ari hadn't found the questions in the least disconcerting. In fact, he couldn't remember the last time his heart had felt so light. It was such a relief not to have to dodge the topic of his bizarre swan years. The princesses might view him with the fascination one would feel for an exotic animal, but at least they didn't find the topic awkward like his own people did.

"So what brings you to Tola, Prince Ari?"

The question came from the young woman sitting next to Ari, and he raised a hand in protest.

"Just Ari, please. I'm sorry, I didn't catch—"

"I'm Princess Violet," she rescued him helpfully, not seeming at all irked that he hadn't remembered her name. "But you can just call me Violet, of course. We met at Basil and Wren's wedding, I think, but I can't say I would have been able to pick you out of your brothers by name."

Ari grinned at her. "Well, that lets me off the hook."

She laughed. "Definitely. You have a much better excuse than I do. Only six of you, and twelve of us. You must feel like you're lost in a stampede."

Ari cast a glance around the table. The meal was in full swing, but the amount of food being consumed hadn't caused any notable drop in the volume. The princess sitting on his other side leaned across the table to feed little Prince Teddy some chicken, and meanwhile the girl on Obsidian's lap was being doted upon by one of the younger girls. Little Princess Azure was still on Wren's lap, while her mother tried with limited success to stop her from putting everything she could get her chubby little hands on into her mouth. Mainly the silverware. Clearly the children were much adored by the family at large.

"It is a lot," he acknowledged. "But I don't mind it. I wish my family was a little more like this, to be honest. I'm the only one who isn't married, and most have children, but even the ones who live in the castle don't have their children join us for meals like this."

"Ah, well there you go," Violet informed him cheerfully. "You're not hard to pick out of the line up at all. Your nieces and nephews can easily remember you—they just need to call you The Uncle Who Can't Land a Wife."

"Thank you for that," said Ari dryly. "Somehow I don't think I'll be suggesting that nickname." He saw she was trying not to laugh, and gave in, grinning himself. "Only because The Unlucky Uncle is much less of a mouthful."

"Unlucky?" she asked solemnly. "Or lucky to have such a clear identifying feature? There are still ten of us sisters in the same situation, and even though Zinnia is married and living out of the castle now, I still frequently get mistaken for her. I'm often told we look particularly alike, and poor Jasmine gets the same." She nodded toward a young teenager halfway down the table.

Ari followed her gaze, thoughtfully assessing both of the sisters identified. "I don't know," he said, his eyes flicking between her and the others a couple of times. The three shared the same wavy brown hair, and there was some similarity of features, but it wasn't a remarkable likeness—neither of them had quite the presence Violet did. "I don't think you look that similar," he announced. "I'll admit I didn't remember your name, but having had a proper conversation with you, I don't think I'd mistake you for either Zinnia or Jasmine. Or for any of your sisters, really."

"Truly?" Violet demanded. She plastered on an expression of mock astonishment, but underneath, Ari thought she was genuinely delighted. "Say no more, handsome prince from a foreign land! Marry me at once!"

"I—?" Ari's inarticulate stutter was cut off by a scandalized voice from Violet's other side.

"Violet! Have you no shame?"

Violet sent a long-suffering look toward the older princess, whom Ari didn't even realize had been listening to their conversation.

"It was a joke, Lilac." Violet's eyes flicked back to Ari, laughter dancing in their depths as she took in his still-blank expression. "Just a joke," she assured him.

"Hardly an appropriate joke," said Lilac tartly. "Honestly, Violet, what will Prince Ari think of us if you carry on in that manner?"

The princess sounded ready to launch into a full lecture,

and Ari could see from Violet's face that none of it would be either new or welcome.

"Of course it was a joke," he cut in smoothly, sending Lilac a smile he hoped would be disarming. "And I never answered your original question, Violet. I'm only passing through Tola. I'm headed for Bansford." He named a kingdom to the east of Entolia. "I've heard a rumor that they're planning an expedition across the desert, and I want to wheedle my way in if possible."

"Across the desert?" asked another of the girls from Ari's other side. "I thought it was impassable."

"It is as far as anyone knows," Ari agreed. "I should have said an expedition *around* the desert, because the rumor is they're going to sail. But I don't know if there's any truth to it. I was itching to go somewhere, so I thought I'd investigate in person."

"It must be wonderful to be that free," said the princess who'd asked Ari about eating worms. "The difference between being a prince and a princess, I suppose."

"Prince Ari is a fully-grown man, Briar," said Lilac. Her exasperated tone perfectly matched the way their mother had chastised the young sister who'd first questioned Ari. "You're sixteen. There's a subtle difference."

Briar responded sharply, and the conversation quickly devolved into a heated but muted argument. Taken aback, Ari glanced around. No one was taking much notice, the general clamor continuing.

"Want to escape?" Violet asked in an undertone.

"Escape?" Ari repeated, bewildered.

She nodded solemnly. "Before Lilac loses interest in lecturing Briar, and returns her attention to us."

"But...can we?" Ari protested. "I mean, won't we be missed?"

"I thought you were a swan, not a chicken," Violet said, completely straight-faced.

Ari narrowed his eyes at her, trying to keep his rising mirth at bay and match her tone. "You'd be wise not to criticize any type of fowl until you've flapped a mile in their feathers. Their lives aren't as idyllic as you might think."

Violet just grinned. "Yes," she said, her voice suddenly a little louder. "These tapestries were commissioned by my grandfather, actually. Let me show you."

Ari followed obediently as she crossed the room. She came to a stop in front of one of a pair of matching tapestries that hung on either side of glass double doors. Through the doors, Ari could see a small patio. Once he was alongside her, Violet threw a glance over her shoulder at the table, then tugged on his sleeve and slipped through the door into the cool night air.

Emerging onto the patio behind her, Ari couldn't help but laugh. "Where are we going, and why are we running away?"

"I'm not running away," Violet said lightly, moving across the patio. "But I'm really not in the mood for one of Lilac's scolds." She shook her head. "I do love her, but she can be insufferable at times. Maybe you're more fortunate in your older siblings, but—"

"I have five older brothers," Ari cut her off flatly. "If you think they're all genial and easygoing, and not one is ever insufferable, you've lost your mind."

Violet chuckled, but she didn't turn back to him. She'd reached the exterior wall of the building, and to Ari's astonishment, she grabbed hold of an ornamental stone dragon's head sticking out of the wall, attempting to pull herself up with it.

"No good." She turned to him. "Give me a boost?"

"A what?" Ari asked, dazed.

"A boost," Violet repeated. "With your hands."

Feeling like he must be dreaming, Ari found himself

clasping his hands together and dropping to one knee. Next thing he knew, Violet had stepped onto his hands and pulled herself up to the dragon's head. She reached for another one, her sights apparently set on a sizable overhang that formed a roof for the patio.

"Where are you going?" Ari asked, bewildered.

"I told you, we're escaping," Violet informed him. "Only if you can keep up, of course."

Ari pulled himself up behind her, unable to resist that challenge. With his longer arms, he had no difficulty reaching the handhold. "I just didn't realize you meant it so literally," he retorted.

He had to admit, he was impressed by her nimbleness as he followed her up the wall and across to the overhang. Soon they were sitting side by side, looking out at the darkness of what appeared to be a small garden.

"Listen," Violet said softly. "Do you hear it?"

Ari stilled, listening. A dull, pulsing roar filled his ears. It was a pleasant sound. "The sea," he murmured. "I've rarely visited the coast. It must be nice to live so near the ocean."

"It is," Violet said simply. She didn't expand, and for a moment they just sat in a companionable silence, eventually broken by a voice drifting out from the room below. Ari recognized it as Princess Lilac's.

"I thought they went out...oh, there's no one here. Perhaps Prince Ari wished to retire early?"

Violet grinned conspiratorially at Ari. "She'll scold me tremendously when I get back to my suite, but that won't take this moment away from me."

"Is your sister really so overbearing you have to actually run away from her?" Ari asked mildly.

Violet sobered. "No, of course not," she said. She sighed, the sound so soft Ari almost missed it. "I'm just a firm believer in the unpredictability of tomorrow. You never know what changes are coming, so it's wise to take advantage of whatever freedom you have now, while you still can."

Ari frowned a little. There was something behind the seemingly light words, something he couldn't quite read. But he didn't press. He found himself quite content to talk of nothing and everything with Violet for another half an hour, before the chill of the night drove them back inside. From Violet's casual demeanor, he was sure the stragglers still in the dining hall assumed they'd been standing on the patio the whole time. Lilac, mercifully, appeared to have retired.

After wishing his sister a dutiful goodnight, Ari hastened to do the same, the weariness of his journey catching up with him at last.

And yet, as he drifted to sleep, he thought neither of the home he'd left nor of any unformed adventures on the other side of the desert. For once, his mind was very much occupied with where he was, and what was in front of him. Specifically, a pair of laughing hazel eyes.

# CHAPTER TWO

# *Violet*

Violet woke slowly, her mind captured by a lingering sense of pleasure she couldn't quite put her finger on. She opened her eyes, taking in the familiar canopy of her bed, and the ocean breeze shifting the curtains. A maid must have opened the window.

Memory returned as Violet sat up, and she smiled to herself. Prince Ari had arrived from Mistra the night before. And she'd let her more reckless side out, driven by the potentially drastic step she intended to take today. She'd felt she had nothing to lose, and every reason to enjoy whatever hijinks she could while opportunity offered. Basil was a much more lenient head of the royal family than her father had been, but she knew not all men ran their households that way.

Looking back over their conversation and her own behavior —brazen, Lilac had called it when Violet returned to her suite to find her sister waiting—she had to acknowledge Ari would have cause to be scandalized.

But he hadn't seemed to mind. If she'd read him correctly, he'd found the chaos of the Entolian royal family overwhelming but not unpleasant. And, by her best guess, he'd had much the same reaction to her.

Violet chuckled to herself as she rose, assessing her own thoughts about the visiting prince. She liked him, she decided. He wasn't quite what she'd expected. Wren was so reserved… Ari was less measured and less sophisticated. He was perfectly well-mannered—more so than she'd been—but there was an impression of frustrated energy underneath, which Wren entirely lacked.

She'd been foolish to expect him to be like Wren, though. As one of thirteen, Violet should know better than anyone not to assume siblings would all be alike in personality.

Yes, she liked Ari, she decided, as she sat down before her looking glass and studied her disheveled locks. He would be a welcome addition to the family circle for the next week. But she'd do well not to let herself like him *too* much. She'd yet to meet anyone who affected her that way, and it would be the worst possible timing for her to find herself attracted to some-one. Especially someone as eligible as a foreign prince.

"Your Highness, you're awake." A servant bustled in from Violet's receiving room, her voice apologetic. "I thought you were still sleeping."

"I just woke," Violet said cheerfully. "No need to rush on my account." She looked the servant over. She wasn't one of Violet's personal maids, but she attended the princess often enough to be familiar. "Naomi, isn't it?"

The maid nodded. "Yes, Your Highness. I've laid out some gowns, if you care to make a selection."

"Thank you." Violet nodded absently, casting her eyes over the gowns laid out on a settee nearby. "The purple one," she said. "And I'll wear my silver set, the simple one with the neck-lace that—oh," she broke off, remembering. "No, I dropped it down the side of the bureau the other week, didn't I?" She sighed. "I must ask Basil about it again."

It was her favorite necklace, and she'd been so frustrated when it slipped from her fingers at the most inopportune moment. The bureau in question was enormous, and affixed to the wall, so it wasn't a matter of getting a few burly servants to shift the furniture. It would require tools, and any alterations to a royal suite had to be approved by the sovereign, she'd discovered.

She'd already mentioned it to Basil three times, but she didn't blame her brother for forgetting. He had so much on his plate, and although he carried his responsibilities amazingly for such a young king, she knew the strain it took on him. Truth be told, that type of request wouldn't have fared much better under her father. She might be a princess, but given she was only one of twelve princesses, she was used to that status providing less indulgence than the average person probably thought.

She would just have to wait, and wear a different necklace until Basil had time to address it. It wasn't exactly a crushing hardship.

"I hope you slept well, Your Highness," Naomi said, as she began to dress Violet's hair.

"Yes, thank you," Violet replied, her mind not on their conversation.

There was a moment of silence before the maid continued, her voice a little hesitant. "You seemed to enjoy dinner last night, Princess Violet. You and Prince Ari appear to be on... extremely good terms."

Violet met the other girl's eyes in the mirror, her attention properly captured. The maid was commenting on her interactions with Ari? That wasn't appropriate. Violet knew gossip ran rife in a castle—among royals and servants alike—and they didn't stand on as much ceremony as some sovereigns did. But for a servant she barely knew to be making sly remarks about potential romances was a little far.

Although Naomi's reflection didn't support the idea that she was teasing Violet, or looking for juicy gossip. Her expression was solemn but searching as it rested on Violet's face, as if hoping to read her thoughts.

She would be disappointed. Violet raised one eyebrow, assuming her most aloof royal air. She was still a princess, after all.

"I'm not sure I understand your implication. Did you anticipate *poor* relations between my family and the family of my sister-in-law, our queen?"

"Of course not, Your Highness," said Naomi, backing down at once. "I meant no disrespect."

Violet continued to regard the maid coolly, but inside she was remembering her conversation with Ari the night before. Had he meant it when he said he wouldn't mistake her for one of her sisters? He'd seemed sincere. He certainly knew how to get into her good graces if so.

Underneath her haughty expression, Violet fought a grin as she pictured Ari's face when she'd jokingly demanded that he marry her. It was all in jest, and he'd clearly taken it as such. Where was the harm in enjoying what freedom she had left? She had an important meeting to attend, but it was a few hours away yet. Perhaps their guest would like a tour.

Violet had overslept, so she wasn't surprised to see her family members trickling out of the dining hall as she approached it. To her delight, Ari's tall form appeared just behind Wren. She took a moment to study him as he unknowingly approached her. His hair was cropped closely, perhaps to prevent it from being as unmanageable as she knew Wren's could be, and his frame was lean, his limbs so long she had no doubt they'd been gangly in his youth. Or would have been, if he hadn't spent his formative years as a swan, she reminded herself.

In any event, he wasn't gangly now. He'd grown into his height, and he moved with a confidence that was appealing, even if his steps bounced with that impression of frustrated energy she'd noted the night before. He was dressed in the more formal style of the Mistrans, but the morning was warm, and he'd rolled his sleeves back to reveal the dark skin of his forearms.

In short, she liked what she saw. Perhaps a little too much.

*Just a bit of harmless flirtation,* she reminded herself lightly. *He's heading off for an adventure in a week, and my future is about to take a different direction.*

Without warning, her breath caught in her throat, and she massaged the feature with one hand, trying to fight off the feeling of suffocation. She gave her head a little shake. She was being foolish. She might be about to make a huge sacrifice for her family and kingdom, but she wasn't literally going to sacrifice herself. It wasn't as though she was dying.

And none of that was the point right now. The point was that neither she nor Ari had anything to lose. If her days of freedom were numbered, it was all the more reason to enjoy them while she could.

"Violet! There you are." Her brother's voice was a welcome interruption to her thoughts, especially since he refrained from chastising her for sleeping through breakfast. A forbearance that made all his sisters love their young king fiercely.

"Morning, Basil," Violet said, trying to inject her usual cheerfulness back into her tone. It helped that she hadn't missed the way Ari had looked up at her name, abandoning his conversation with Wren. Violet nodded to her brother's wife. "Wren. Where are the children?"

"With the nursemaid," Wren said, smiling at her. "Did you sleep well?"

"Of course," said Violet lightly.

"And you haven't forgotten the meeting with the Merchants' Guild today?" Wren added.

"I remember," Violet assured her more seriously. "I'll be there."

Basil frowned. "I'm sorry, Vi, I really am. It'll be unbearably dull. You really shouldn't have to sit through every single complaint they—"

"Don't try to talk her out of her role, after we had to bully you for so long to let her assume it in the first place," Wren scolded her husband gently. "You can't do *everything* yourself, Basil. And Violet's been doing an excellent job of liaising with the guild on your behalf."

"Of course you have," Basil told Violet, still looking apologetic. "I just wish you didn't have to."

Violet gave him a long-suffering look. "Basil, Wren is right. Stop trying to carry the whole kingdom alone. What's the use of all these younger siblings if you won't let us lighten your load? You need me there. I've been your go-between on this for months, and you're going to want my input. Trust me."

"I do," Basil assured her.

"If you want to repay me," said Violet jokingly, "authorize the steward to send a team to my suite to remove the bureau and rescue my favorite necklace."

Basil slapped a hand to his head. "I forgot. You asked me that already, didn't you? Sorry, Violet. I'll speak to him today."

Violet waved off her brother's apology. She knew he meant it, and it wasn't that he was an unreliable person. But she doubted such an insignificant domestic matter would actually stay in his head once he reached his study and was confronted with kingdom-wide issues. She didn't blame him.

"The meeting with the guild isn't for hours, though," she said, turning to Ari. The Mistran had stood silently throughout the exchange. "I wondered if Ari would like a tour of the castle in the meantime?"

"Did you?" Wren sounded faintly amused.

Violet gave a solemn nod, her eyes on Ari's face. He looked pleased, but wary. Clearly she'd succeeded in keeping him guessing, if nothing else.

"Yes," she said innocently. "I thought he might get bored in the company of a dull old married couple."

"Did you?" Basil echoed his wife's words, the look he sent Violet telling her he wasn't quite as forbearing regarding her flirtation as he was about her tardiness.

Violet just grinned at him before turning to Ari. "What do you say, Ari?"

"I'm at your disposal, Princess," Ari said, his lips twitching.

"Excellent," she said brightly, inclining her head in the opposite direction to where Wren and Basil were walking. Ari followed her, keeping up easily with his longer stride.

"What's the meeting with the Merchants' Guild about?" he asked curiously, once they'd left the others behind.

"Oh, nothing of consequence," said Violet, her light tone unconvincing even in her own ears. In her defense, it wasn't easy to speak casually of an event which was quite possibly going to determine the course of her entire life. If the meeting went as she feared and expected, her fate was all but sealed.

But she didn't say any of this to Ari. Instead she just sent him a tight smile. "Nothing we need concern ourselves with, anyway."

"I'd hate for anything to interrupt the all-important tour," Ari agreed. He sent her an amused look. "You do remember that I've been here before, don't you? I received a very official tour before Wren and Basil's wedding."

Violet shrugged a shoulder. "Yes, but official tours are horridly dull. And not very informative." She raised an eyebrow in challenge. "Can you remember a single fact you were told on that tour?"

"No," Ari confessed. "Not a single one."

"Precisely." Violet nodded sagely. "My tour will be much more interesting. For starters—" she pointed down an adjoining corridor as they passed, "that storeroom down there is where the housekeeper once discovered half a dozen serving men indulging in a whole barrel of ale they'd taken from the kitchens the night of a gala. They were all promptly dismissed." Her voice took on a reminiscent tone. "That was in my father's time. There are much more scandalous stories about my grandfather's rule."

"Spare my sensibilities, I beg of you," Ari said in mock horror.

"I shan't," Violet informed him brutally. "I promised you an interesting tour, and that's what you'll get. I should really take you to the gardens for the full circuit, but they're on the other side of the castle and not at all in our route."

"What's in the gardens?" Ari asked curiously.

"A secret tunnel," Violet said with relish.

"Really?" Ari demanded.

She nodded. "It hasn't been used for a long time, and hardly anyone remembers it anymore. Even if they did, it wouldn't matter, as the end is sealed up. My sisters and I used to play in it when we were little. But its original purpose was quite scandalous. Apparently my grandfather's brother was a little...loose, and he had it built so he could sneak women into the castle."

"Sounds like a security risk," Ari commented.

Violet nodded again. "It was. That's why it was all boarded up." She sent him a sideways grin. "We weren't even supposed to know about it, but Zinnia and I found it once, when we were hiding from one of our tutors. The poor deluded man wanted us to study geography when the sun was shining in the sky, can you believe it?"

Ari matched her grin with one of his own. "He doesn't sound nearly intelligent enough to be a royal tutor."

Violet chuckled. "If I really want to offend you, I could tell all sorts of details about the stories the gossips used to tell about the Mistrans in the years before and during the war."

As she spoke, she looked up and caught sight of an unfamiliar man, watching them from a nearby doorway with a frown on his face. As soon as he realized she was looking, he smoothed out his expression and dipped his head. She inclined hers in response, wondering who he was.

Ari must have noticed that she'd stopped speaking, because he looked over as well, his face brightening in recognition.

"Lex. Is all well?"

"Yes, Your Highness," the man responded. "I've just been checking on our horses. All in excellent form."

"Very good," said Ari cheerfully. "Lex, this is Princess Violet. Violet, Lex is one of my family's oldest and most faithful servants."

Violet greeted him politely, unable to help noticing that while his manner was the height of polite respect, his expression never fully softened.

After a moment the pair moved on, and Violet waited until they were well out of the man's earshot before speaking again.

"I was likely insensitive with my earlier comment," she said. "About all the gossip regarding Mistrans and their terrible ways."

"Not at all," said Ari, his voice dry. She shot him a sideways look, and he smiled in return. "I doubt your tales would be as impressive as you think. I could match them and then some, I imagine. Entolians weren't well-regarded in Mistra back then."

"And probably still aren't for many, if your servant is anything to go by," Violet said lightly. "He's the one I suspect found my comment insensitive. It's all right," she added quickly, seeing Ari's discomfort. "I understand it. We grew up thinking our people were enemies, didn't we? We've had years of Wren's presence to rid ourselves of that notion, but those in Myst haven't had the same advantage."

Ari said nothing, probably too polite to confirm it. He glanced around, confusion crossing his features as Violet led him through an external doorway.

"Why are we outside?" he asked. "I thought you were showing me around the castle."

Violet waved a careless hand at the stone building behind her. "There it is. It's very nice, we like it."

Ari chuckled. "Where are you really taking me? Should I have brought my guards? Should I rally Lex to come to my aid?"

"Only if you think you can't beat me in a fight," Violet responded with a grin. "I'm giving you the real tour. You haven't seen our castle if you haven't spent time on the cliffs. This is where we prefer to be, as much as we can."

They had crossed a small courtyard while she spoke, and a moment later made their way through a gate manned by armed guards. Ari blinked at the vista before him, looking surprised as he grasped that they'd left the city itself. The sudden fierceness of the wind should have been as big a clue as the sight of the grassy hills ahead and the ocean to one side. In this part of the capital, the wall of the castle formed the city wall itself.

"Zinnia and Obsidian's place is up that way," Violet informed her companion, raising her voice against the wind as she gestured further along the cliff. "And this is our favorite haunt."

Ari said nothing as he followed her along the well-worn track to the cliff's edge. After only a short distance, they reached the cliff face, and the familiar winding path down was revealed. Violet led the way, her ears telling her that Ari wasn't far behind. Once they reached the relative shelter of the beach below, she smiled at him, pleased not to have to yell now they were off the windy clifftop.

"It's nice being grown, and not being required to bring minders in order to leave the castle." Her smile grew cheeky. "I'll have to depend on you to protect me in the event of danger."

Ari laughed. "I'll do my best to serve as chivalry demands," he assured her. His eyes strayed to the water, and Violet could see his fascination. "I'm afraid I would be more likely to be the one needing rescuing, given how unfamiliar I am with the ocean."

"It is mesmerizing, isn't it?" Violet said, following his gaze. She was well pleased with what she'd seen in his eyes. Tola was the only capital in the continent of Solstice to be situated on the coast, so she'd played guide to many visitors experiencing the seaside for the first time. In her experience, people were either immediately captivated by the ocean's beauty and mystery, or they weren't. And if they weren't, there was simply no explaining it to them. It had to be felt. And harsh as it might sound to those who hadn't grown up with the ocean such a central and beloved part of their lives, anyone who couldn't feel it wasn't her kind of person.

Not that there was any need for Ari to be her kind of person, she reminded herself. This was all just a bit of foolish fun, and it shouldn't matter in the least whether he was naturally receptive to the lure of the sea, and all it represented.

But somehow, it did matter.

"I spent half my childhood here," she commented, keen to talk herself out of her reflective mood. "So did all my sisters. Poor Basil was never as free to roam as the rest of us were, but truth be told, most in the castle were pleased to have us down here and out from underfoot. Twelve is a lot of princesses to navigate."

Ari smiled. "I can imagine. I thought we had a large family with seven of us. I have no idea how poor little Teddy and Azure are going to remember the names of all their aunts and uncles." His eyes skimmed over the choppy water with its white caps, settling on the horizon. "I can see why you all liked to be here rather than cooped up inside, though. There's something almost magical about the ocean, isn't there?"

"There is," Violet agreed happily. "They say even dragons all have a longing for the sea, so perhaps there is some magic about it." She could hear her own voice turn a little sad. "Dragons used to come here quite often. Two in particular were friends of ours, to an extent. But we haven't seen them in years. Not since…"

Her voice trailed off, and Ari finished the thought, his own words calm. "Since your curse was lifted."

Violet shot him a sharp look, and he raised one eyebrow. "What, you're allowed to tease me about being a swan for six years, but I'm not allowed to mention the fact that you and all your sisters were under a crushing curse of your own?"

Violet couldn't help laughing, even as she grimaced in concession of his point. "It wasn't that crushing," she told him frankly. "Not at the time, at least, only afterward. Well," she amended, "it was pretty awful for Zinnia all along. But that's ancient history now. We're free of malicious curses, at least as far as I'm aware."

"Yes, I'm ready to never encounter magic again," Ari said.

Violet sent him an amused smile. "Don't let Obsidian hear you say that." She tilted her head to the side. "Actually, he wouldn't take offense. He's not at all puffed up about magic the way they are at the Enchanters' Guild. It can be handy having a brother-in-law who can work magic, though." Her eyes lit up as a thought occurred to her. "Maybe I should ask *him* to help get my necklace back! I hadn't thought of that. I'll have to try to corner him next time he's in the castle."

Ari squinted at her. "The necklace that requires a bureau to be moved?"

"Yes," said Violet, surprised that he'd taken note of her idle comment to Basil. Banishing the inconsequential matter from her mind, she turned her face back to the ocean, and her conversation to more interesting points.

"Since I have you alone, Ari..." She looked up to see him watching her with a suddenly wary expression, and couldn't resist indulging in a grin before letting him off the hook. "I have questions for you. We love Wren as our own, but she's maddeningly poised. Please tell me you have some embarrassing stories about her from childhood. I need something in my arsenal."

Ari relaxed, letting out a laugh that was appealingly deep. "There I can certainly help you," he assured her. "Although I might require some about Basil in return."

They passed the next hour in good-natured ribbing of their siblings, and Violet found herself reluctant to return to the castle. But it wouldn't do to be late to the meeting with the Merchants' Guild. On the contrary, she was determined to be the first in the room, to better observe everyone as they entered, and get a sense of which way the wind blew. Perhaps tempers would be improved since their last discussion, she thought optimistically. Perhaps it wouldn't be necessary for her to take any drastic steps.

The thought was more welcome than it should have been, even though she knew she was grasping at straws. Unease stirred in Violet's core as they walked back up the cliff path. Not long ago, she'd been able to remain fairly detached toward her scheme. But now, every step she took closer to her plan felt like walking on blades.

Somehow she'd let emotion enter into the equation, and it was doing her no favors. In fact, if she didn't get herself together, it could very well break her heart.

# CHAPTER THREE

## *Violet*

Violet thought Ari seemed regretful when she took her leave of him, but she forced her thoughts away from him and toward the task at hand. By the time the various attendees arrived, Violet was settled in a seat in the small audience chamber, next to the place set aside for Basil.

She'd expected Basil to be last, knowing he had another meeting beforehand, but he surprised her by slipping in next to her as the first of the guild members arrived.

"Violet," he greeted her.

She nodded at him, noticing as she did so that Wren was taking the seat on his other side. Violet bit her lip.

"Is it a good idea for Wren to be here?"

"Of course," said Basil calmly. "Wren is my wife and our kingdom's queen. Her presence will always be appropriate in discussing matters of import to our state."

Violet gave him a look, not bothering to call out his intentional misunderstanding of her question. She didn't try to talk him out of his view, as she knew there would be no point. Basil was inflexible in regard to his wife. She applauded his attitude for the most part, but she hoped it wouldn't serve them badly in the negotiations to come. Basil was the best of brothers and clearly an excellent husband, but not known for his tact.

"How bad do you think it's going to get?" he asked her in an undertone.

Violet sighed as she watched a group of men file into the room, one particular merchant at their head.

"Pretty bad," she said frankly. "Ulrich doesn't look happy."

Basil's eyes followed hers, and he calmly regarded the man entering the room. Ulrich was the head of Entolia's wealthiest merchant family, and ran the Merchants' Guild both in name and in practice. He was incredibly influential among the other merchants, and he wasn't happy with the sovereign at present. To put it mildly.

"I'm glad he's brought his son," Basil murmured, his eyes on the young man beside Ulrich. "The younger generation can sometimes be more reasonable."

Another pang of sharp emotion went through Violet at the sight of the young man. Where was the detachment she so desperately needed now? But she kept her many thoughts to herself, giving only a non-committal grunt. She'd had much more interaction with the pair than Basil, and while she had no reason to ascribe any malicious intent to the younger man, she doubted he would see eye to eye with Basil. In her experience, the members of the Merchants' Guild were interested in profit, not in the broader well-being of the kingdom. That was the king's job, after all.

"What's his son's name again?" Basil asked.

"Yannick," she said, just as the men took their seats. The name tasted sour in her mouth, and she sternly told herself to stop being dramatic.

Basil stood, and everyone else did the same. He waved them down with a casual hand.

"Welcome, and thank you all for attending," he said. "I

anticipate fruitful discussion today. I'm ready to hear your grievances, and I have information to share with you as well. I trust with open communication, we can reach a satisfactory resolution to our impasse."

"Indeed, Your Majesty?" said Ulrich, his tone of respect so forced it was painful. "Are we to understand then that you've given orders for the Mistran merchants to cease trading in Tola immediately?"

Violet wanted to scowl at the older man. She'd watched Basil take this kind of disrespect from men of generations above ever since he was crowned at eighteen. And he took it with excellent grace. But it never failed to infuriate her. Still, she followed his lead and held her peace.

"You know I have not, Ulrich," said Basil calmly, taking his seat. "And I don't have any intention of doing anything so absolute. But that doesn't mean we can't put safeguards in place to protect the interests of our Entolian merchants."

"Ours are the *only* interests you should be protecting, Your Majesty," cut in another merchant, as irate as Ulrich. "You have no obligation to the Mistrans—and you've allowed them to take over our markets!"

"They've done nothing of the kind," said Basil patiently. "And it's not accurate to say there is no obligation to Mistra, as I know you're aware."

"We have the records to prove how significantly our trade has suffered since you gave the Mistrans open access to Entolian markets," contradicted Ulrich. "We never agreed to any alliance. Your choice of wife is costing us our livelihood, Your Majesty."

Basil rose to his feet, the movement slow and controlled, but every line of his lean frame radiating authority. Begrudgingly, everyone else stood as well.

"My marriage is not open for discussion, Ulrich," he said,

the calm words more compelling than shouting would have been.

Violet noticed a number of the men sneaking looks at Wren, Ulrich's expression openly dark. The young queen took it with her usual grace, but Violet found herself frowning on her sister-in-law's behalf. Personal considerations aside, Ulrich's claims were far from true. Mistran merchants were allowed to trade in Entolia since the war ended, it was true. But they hadn't been given a free pass. Regulations were in place. Besides which, she knew from her own research that the man's livelihood was in no danger. He was excessively wealthy.

"I remain of the view that the benefits of open trade with Mistra outweigh the costs," Basil said, lowering the intensity of his voice. His eyes found Ulrich's sole son and heir. "Yannick, do you have any reflections on this point? You visited Myst not long ago, I believe? Did you not observe the benefits of open trade with Mistra?"

Yannick took a moment to respond, seeming reluctant to be drawn out. "It was an informative visit, Your Majesty," he said finally. "Entolian merchants were engaged in trade, certainly, and much of it very profitable. But I did observe some discrimination directed toward them from the local merchants."

"I suspect it was nothing beyond the discrimination Mistran merchants have faced in Tola, from members of this guild," Violet interjected.

"Violet is right," Basil said. If he was disappointed that Yannick hadn't been more of an ally, he didn't show it. At least the younger man was much calmer than his father, showing no inclination to rage at the king or the Mistrans. "And I'd like to take this opportunity to remind everyone that before the war, there was trade between us and our neighbors—long before the marriage alliance between myself and Queen Wren."

He resumed his seat. "Nevertheless, I've come prepared to hear your grievances, as I indicated."

As Violet had known they would, those words opened floodgates which couldn't be closed for the rest of the afternoon. For hours they sat in the room listening to the disgruntled merchants, occasionally managing to speak themselves, only to have every point disregarded. From what Violet could tell, they were making no progress at all, unless moving backwards counted.

When the word embargo was spoken aloud, Basil called the meeting to a halt. The afternoon was wearing toward evening and even Basil's usual calm was visibly wearing thin.

"Sorry, Violet," Basil said wearily, as the merchants filed out of the room. "It looks like I'm subjecting you to another day of this."

Violet frowned at her brother. "What are you apologizing for?" she scolded. "This mess isn't of your making."

"No, but it's still my mess to fix," Basil said. He gave her a rueful smile. "And I'm doing a poor job of that."

"No you're not," Wren contradicted, and Violet agreed.

"Do you have any ideas on how to break the deadlock?" she asked her brother, trying to keep the hint of desperation from her voice. This was her last chance for a way out, and she had no real expectation of rescue. "Anything I don't know about?"

Basil shook his head. "To be perfectly frank, I don't know how to proceed. Ulrich is the real problem." He looked sharply at her. "Am I right in thinking that he has almost absolute influence in the guild?"

Violet nodded. "Unfortunately, yes. The rest will follow him, even if he goes through with the embargo idea. And I'm afraid he's not a very reasonable man. His ego is too big to allow for that. Nothing but his way will be good enough."

"And he's decided that the only way he'll accept is a

complete ban on Mistran merchants in Tola, which is completely unreasonable," Basil sighed.

Wren looked troubled. "Would the Merchants' Guild really carry out an embargo on their own city? Surely if they lose all trade within Tola, they'll be the ones to come out worse?"

"Depends how long the embargo held," said Violet unemotionally. "If it succeeded, and Basil yielded, they would regain all the business they've lost to the Mistran merchants."

"Well, I won't yield," Basil said flatly.

Violet said nothing. Basil's attitude wasn't news to her. And while she wouldn't wish to see her brother give in to such demands as Ulrich was making, if things proceeded as they were, she could foresee nothing but hardship for everyone involved—and the regular people of the capital would suffer the most.

"I'll speak with Ulrich again before the next meeting," she said. "Perhaps there is a way to reason with him."

She didn't wait for a response, slipping from the room as Basil and Wren continued their debrief in low voices. Her feet were reluctant, as if determined to convince her she was racing toward her own doom, but she forced them into motion. If she hurried, she could catch Ulrich and his son before they left the castle.

Sure enough, they were just crossing the broad entranceway when she reached them. Father and son both turned at her greeting, Ulrich still clearly irate, and Yannick's face giving little away.

"Your Highness," said Ulrich stiffly.

"I wish to speak with you both," Violet said, pleased that her voice was steady. "Would you step into the courtyard with me?"

"Can the matter not wait until tomorrow's meeting, Your Highness?" Ulrich asked, not very graciously.

"I'm hoping that tomorrow's meeting may not be necessary once you've heard my proposal," Violet said.

The two men exchanged glances, clearly intrigued. With a word to the rest of his retinue, Ulrich moved toward Violet. She led them not outside, but further into the building, to an internal courtyard that had been decorated in an ocean theme. An artificial pond graced the center of the space, resembling a tide pool with its sandy bottom and seashells. Violet didn't lower herself onto one of the carved stone benches, preferring to remain standing as she turned to her audience.

"You said you had a proposal for us, Your Highness?" Ulrich prompted. "What did you mean by that?"

"Exactly that," Violet said, laying one hand on a decorative ship's wheel for an anchor. Her head was spinning a little, and she felt strangely adrift, but she wasn't going to turn back now. Basil needed help, and for the first time in her life she had the power to come to his aid. Her eyes strayed to Yannick, then back to Ulrich. "I understand your concerns regarding the Mistran merchants."

"So you agree about the undesirability of—"

"No." Violet cut off Ulrich's eager words. "I do not share your view on the matter itself. But I understand your concern about the loss of both income and status. To speak frankly—"

"When does any member of your family do anything else?" Ulrich muttered audibly.

Violet gave a grim smile but didn't otherwise respond. "To speak frankly," she started again, "I wondered whether a guarantee regarding the retention of your current influence in the guild and the broader community might be enough to reconcile you to the potential loss of income."

Ulrich raised an eyebrow. "And how do you propose to *guarantee* my influence?"

Violet transferred her gaze to Yannick. "Through you," she

told him bluntly. "I'm not spoken for, and unless I've been misinformed, neither are you. I'm proposing a marriage of political advantage. I trust you won't think me arrogant when I express the view that marrying a princess will ensure—and indeed increase—your family's influence."

For a moment there was silence, Ulrich looking stunned and Yannick thoughtful.

"What do you think?" Violet prompted at last, her eyes on Yannick, but the question mainly intended for Ulrich.

"I think we would be honored to be allied with your esteemed royal house," Ulrich said. "Since you've been direct, may I be the same? Is this idea sanctioned by His Majesty?"

"The idea is mine, not Basil's," Violet said. "But you can rest easy that my brother will not interfere in my choice of groom. He's made his feelings on his sisters' autonomy in that area clear."

"Well, then." Ulrich looked like he was refraining from rubbing his hands together. His reaction was confirming Violet's impression that his protests were more about ego even than profit. "Yannick, what do you say?"

Yannick studied Violet thoughtfully for a moment before replying. "I say that I am flattered, of course, Your Highness. But I confess that you've taken me by surprise. Could I have some time to think on the matter?"

"What is there to think on, Yannick?" Ulrich started, but Violet raised a hand.

"Of course you can. I understand that my proposal is unexpected. We can discuss it further when you've had a chance to reflect."

"Thank you, Your Highness," Yannick said. "You're very gracious."

Violet drew a breath. "I think it best, however, that we all agree not to mention the matter to anyone until a decision has been made."

"I agree," said Yannick at once. He turned to his father. "In any event, we can surely postpone tomorrow's meeting?"

"Yes," agreed Ulrich, looking like he was mentally spending the metaphorical currency of his royal connection already. "I will notify His Majesty."

"Very good," Violet agreed. "I will leave you to reflect." She inclined her head, her eyes searching Yannick's face quickly before she turned for the door. His expression was hooded, clearly deep in thought. No smile lurked in his eyes, but neither did he look displeased. He was hard to read, as she'd noted before now.

Violet's steps were steady as she strode from the room, but her mind was as uneven as the rolling deck of a ship. For some reason, all she could think about was the evening before, particularly her joking words to Ari. *Say no more, handsome prince from a foreign land! Marry me at once!* The thought flashed through her mind that she'd now proposed to two men in as many days. Perhaps Lilac was right, and she was brazen.

She didn't feel brazen, or even confident, in spite of her bold front. She simply felt...weary. And her one desire was to reach the privacy of her room before she succumbed to the uncharacteristic bout of tears threatening to burst at any moment.

# CHAPTER FOUR

# Ari

Ari was embarrassed by how eager he was to get to dinner after being entertained for the afternoon by the dowager queen and her eldest daughter, Princess Lilac.

Not that he couldn't handle a few dull hours. As a prince he was well used to tedium. But he hadn't come to Tola to get to know Princess Lilac and her mother. He'd been hoping to spend time with Wren, and was disappointed that she'd been needed in the meeting with the Merchants' Guild. Even his niece and nephew were otherwise occupied, having been taken to their nursery to nap.

Also—the true source of his embarrassment—he couldn't stop thinking about how much less satisfactory his new hostesses' company was than Violet's. He wasn't sure whether he was attracted to her, or just fascinated by her. But he did know that he wanted to find out more.

To his disappointment, although Violet greeted him in a friendly manner, she didn't sit next to him this time. Nor did she attempt to re-start their banter from earlier. She spoke cheerfully enough to everyone present, himself included, but watching her throughout the meal, he had a strong sense that she was uncomfortable.

Was she regretting their, well, flirtation? There was no other word for it. Ari couldn't help feeling a hint of embarrassment. At least it was private embarrassment, as no one else seemed to have caught the change. In fact, he could see no sign that anyone else had noticed Violet's more subdued demeanor. Much of the meal was occupied with a lively debate initiated by the two youngest sisters in the family—Ivy and Wisteria—who at the age of eight and nine were dissatisfied with still being required to ride smaller, more docile mounts than their fully grown sisters.

Ari didn't pay much attention to the conversation, and to his eye, neither did Violet. Halfway through the meal one of the other sisters—Briar, he thought—moved from her seat beside Violet to speak to her brother about something. Impulsively, Ari pushed his own chair out, embracing the informality of the group and carrying his plate to sit beside Violet. She didn't even look up as he lowered himself into the place beside her.

"Good evening again."

His quiet greeting brought her head snapping up, confusion on her face as she took in his new position.

"Ari. I'm sorry, I didn't see you. How was your afternoon?"

"Fine," said Ari, searching her face. "Are you all right, Violet?"

She blinked at him. "Of course I am. What makes you ask that?"

Ari's face creased in a small frown as he studied her. "*You* do," he said simply. "You don't quite seem yourself."

Violet gave a light laugh. "Bold words for someone who's known me such a short time. Are you an expert on human behavior?"

Ari smiled, relaxing a little at the restoration of her usual bright manner. "Hardly. You just seemed...heavy."

Violet regarded him for a moment, then her face softened into a smile. "You're right, I'm poor company. I must do better. I suppose it would be unkind of me to expect you to carry the conversation since in your own words, your thoughts are no more elevated than those of a swan."

"Swans are very intelligent, I'll have you know," Ari informed her haughtily.

Violet grinned. "Thus confirming the suggestion that you were the issue rather than the swan form."

Ari laughed, lifting his hands in surrender. "All right, I acknowledge. I'm disgracing my kingdom with my lack of wit. I hope Entolia won't withdraw from our alliance knowing what poor stock we provide."

"Nonsense," said Violet, her voice a little sharper than usual. "We're all fully committed to the alliance."

"Of course," said Ari, surprised. "It was a joke."

Violet nodded, seeming to regret her reaction. "I know it was. So what did you do this afternoon while I was stuck in the dullest meeting in history?"

"I had a fairly dull meeting of my own," Ari said. "With Lord Golding, who came with me from Myst. And after that, your mother and Lilac kept me company."

Violet laughed. "So your afternoon was no more exciting than mine. At least they won't have interrogated you about your swan-life."

Ari shook his head with a smile. "I wouldn't have minded if they had," he informed her. "Everyone back home is very awkward about it. I wish people would ask more, if it would remove the general impression that my brothers and I need to be handled with care due to our unnatural affliction."

"No chance of that kind of special treatment here," Violet

told him solemnly. "As you've pointed out, having suffered under a curse doesn't make you remarkable around here."

"No need to think I'm special, got it," Ari responded.

Violet grinned. "Exactly." She studied him. "Do you ever miss it? Being a swan, I mean?"

Ari put his fork down, taken aback by the question. No one had ever asked him that before. "You know..." he said, thinking it over, "I do sometimes. Not being trapped. That was awful. And I'm not saying I wish I could go back or anything. But...I do miss being able to fly. That was pretty great."

"Ooh, that would be amazing," Violet agreed, her eyes lighting up. "I can't even imagine it. None of us got anything like that. Well, Basil was carried by a dragon once, but he said it was more of a stomach-emptying experience than a heart-soaring one."

Ari laughed. "Well, my version of flying was much more pleasant than that. I was very graceful as a swan, if I say so myself."

Violet was so delighted with this description, Ari wondered if he'd come to regret giving himself the compliment. But her banter didn't really trouble him. They passed the rest of the meal in cheerful conversation, Violet showing no sign of her earlier subdued demeanor. Ari could almost have thought he'd imagined it, at least until Violet rose to leave, then paused and turned back to him.

"Ari, about tonight. Thank you."

"For what?" Ari asked, confused.

"For...I don't know." Violet rubbed her neck in the first self-conscious gesture Ari had ever seen from her. "For noticing me, I suppose."

Ari said nothing, unsure how to respond, and with a final smile, Violet swept toward the door. Ari made his way to his own chambers more slowly. For the second night in a row, he fell asleep contemplating Violet, this time trying in vain to read in memory the change in her demeanor which he'd been unable to make sense of at the time.

---

Ari awoke to a loud banging on the door. His groggy eyes fell on a ray of sunlight across the floor that told him that not only had dawn come, but the morning was advanced enough for the servants to have been in and opened the curtains.

He sat up, running a hand through his hair as he tried to get his bearings. The banging had paused, to be replaced with a cheerful call from a voice that was somehow already becoming familiar.

"Wake up, Mistra! This is no time for lying abed. The sun is shining, and it's a sea bathing kind of day!"

"Violet?" Ari muttered, still disoriented.

Someone bustled past him, tutting disapprovingly, and Ari recognized Lex as the servant crossed into the suite's receiving room, from which the banging had come. From the sound of it, Lex opened the room's outer door, speaking to someone still in the corridor.

"I beg your pardon, Your Highness," he said with a courteous tone that still managed to be disapproving. "But Prince Ari is not yet receiving visitors."

"It's all right, Lex," yawned Ari, pushing himself up. "I'm awake. Tell her I'll be ready shortly."

The servant passed the message along dutifully, shutting the door with a firm click before reappearing in Ari's sleeping chamber.

"The royal family allows its young people a great deal of freedom in Entolia," he said, his lips pursed slightly.

Ari grinned, already rummaging through the garments he'd

brought to find the best option for sea bathing. "You say that as though freedom is a bad thing, Lex. I like it. If I had my way, life would always be like this."

"What do you mean, Your Highness?" Lex asked sharply. "You wish to stay in Entolia indefinitely? Surely not."

"No," said Ari, surprised. "I didn't mean that. I just meant that I wish life back home was more relaxed."

The servant looked only slightly mollified, but Ari disregarded the other Mistran's offended pride for his homeland. He was too caught up in pondering Lex's suggestion. The idea of actually living in Entolia hadn't occurred to him, and his logic told him it was foolish to even consider it. Even if Basil and Wren were willing to accept his presence permanently, what justification could he give for staying?

A cheerful and slightly freckled face, surrounded by waves of brown hair, flashed through his mind.

He banished the thought. He was being absurd. He wasn't in Tola to stay. He wasn't even making a long visit. He was there for a week before traveling on to Bansford and hopefully beyond.

Still, he couldn't help the spring of excitement in his step as he emerged from his suite and went in search of Violet. He caught up with her in the small courtyard at the castle's eastern entrance, on the way to the cliffs and the beach below. Most of the family seemed to be gathered there for the outing. He was surprised to see Basil standing next to Violet, not having expected the king to have time for such indulgences. But as he approached, he realized Basil was just speaking with his sister before the group departed.

"So we won't have a meeting with the guild today after all. I won't deny I'm glad to get out of it, but I'm not sure why the change. Ulrich's message just said that on reflection the guild was satisfied with the discussion for the moment and wishes to spend more time coming up with suggestions for a way forward." The young king ran a hand down his chin, his forehead creased in thought. "I don't know whether that's a good sign or a bad one."

"A good one, I'm sure," said Violet firmly. "I think you can give yourself permission to put this particular crisis from your mind for now, Basil. There will be time enough to deal with it when the guild comes back."

The young king smiled ruefully, his expression seeming to say, *If only I could*. But he said no more about it, just wishing the group a pleasant outing. Ari felt for his brother-in-law. He knew that Basil was committed to sitting down with Lord Golding that morning, to discuss various matters Ari's parents had requested the nobleman to communicate. No doubt Basil would prefer to be going swimming with his siblings. There were definite advantages to being the youngest of six brothers.

The experience of sea bathing was new for Ari, and he thoroughly enjoyed it. It didn't hurt that Violet was once again the cheerful, cheeky girl he'd been so intrigued by his first night in Tola. There was a great deal of splashing and squealing, from the grown members of the party as well as the children, and Violet was as bad as any of them. He hung on to the concept of chivalry until the third time she managed to dunk him under, at which point he realized it was utterly wasted on the incorrigible princess. The next time she came for him, he managed to get her first, which only seemed to delight her more. A few times Ari caught one of the other princesses watching their interactions with a little too much interest, but he couldn't bring himself to care. If Violet's behavior had seemed faintly subdued the night before, her actions in the light of day savored of recklessness. And apparently Ari had caught it.

That day it was sea bathing. The next it was horseback riding. The day after, Violet talked him into archery practice in the training yard. Somehow, without any pointed intention, the others in Violet's family lost interest in their plans, and the group activities became one-on-one occasions. Ari found himself passing most of every day with Violet, his intention to spend quality time with his sister fading from his mind.

The other thing that was rapidly fading was his interest in traveling on to Bansford and exploring what might be beyond the desert. He was less inclined to leave by the day, and there was no denying the reason. The fascination Violet provoked didn't lessen the more time he spent with her. Her effervescent presence was as fresh and bracing as the ocean breeze that was a constant part of life in the Entolian castle.

He knew she was flirting shamelessly with him—the disapproving looks she regularly received from her sister Lilac confirmed it—but he didn't mind in the least. How could he, when he lost no opportunity to do the same? Occasionally Violet succumbed once again to the melancholy he'd observed that night at dinner, but whenever he asked her about it, she denied it cheerfully and perked up again. He felt arrogant to think it, but he found himself wondering—even hoping—that the source of her low spirits might be his imminent departure.

The day before he was due to leave, he went in search of Violet only to be told by a servant that she was otherwise engaged by prior appointment. Ari was just making his way back through the castle, feeling foolish for how much the information disappointed him, when her familiar voice caught his ears.

He looked up to see Violet striding down the corridor, apparently giving a tour of some kind. It didn't sound nearly as entertaining as the tour she'd given him, but the young man accompanying her was looking around him with great interest anyway.

Ari frowned at the pair. He'd never seen the man before,

and there was something about his air of confidence that rubbed Ari the wrong way. His eyes slid to Violet, and his frown deepened. She was uncomfortable, her demeanor reminiscent of that night at dinner. It was hard to put his finger on what told him that, but he was sure of it. She was ill at ease.

As Ari watched, Violet led the young man into what appeared to be a meeting room. The stranger paused in the doorway, his eyes flicking around once again and landing on Ari. For a moment the two men regarded each other in silence, then the stranger followed Violet into the room, and a guard closed the door behind them.

Ari turned away, troubled. After a moment's reflection, he went in search of Wren. With his planned departure so close, he'd been feeling guilty for neglecting his sister in favor of spending so much time with Violet. A helpful servant directed him to a garden on the northern side of the castle, which he'd never entered before. It must be the garden Violet had mentioned to him in her initial tour, although she hadn't bothered to actually take him there.

It was a very pleasant spot, sheltered from the ocean by the building. Well-tended garden beds sported blooms of all colors, and trees waved gently in the breeze, rather than being pummeled by the ocean wind.

It was the closest thing he'd seen in Entolia to the garden that graced the center of their castle back home. The garden in which Wren had practically lived for six years, and Ari had literally lived for six years, during his time as a swan. It was no wonder Wren liked this spot.

He found her sitting by a willow, at the edge of a large pond. Little Teddy was kneeling at the water's edge, and Azure was on Wren's lap. Wren seemed to be trying, yet again, to stop her daughter from shoving things in her mouth—this time, a half-rotten, moss-covered stick.

"Ari," Wren greeted him with a smile when he approached. "Have you come to join us? What a rare delight."

There was a twinkle in her eyes as she said it, but Ari still grimaced in acknowledgment of the criticism. "Sorry, Wren."

She waved a hand. "No need to apologize."

Ari sank onto the grass beside her. "There is, though," he said. "I've barely spent time with you, and I'm supposed to be leaving tomorrow."

Wren said nothing, and Ari found himself pulling out blades of grass and rubbing them between his thumb and finger.

"Although, on that topic," he added casually, "I've been toying with the idea of extending my time here. If you wouldn't object."

He snuck a glance at his sister to see that she was fighting a smile. He narrowed his eyes at her. She was a year younger than him—when had she gained the air of an indulgent older sibling? Probably when she became a mother.

"You're very welcome to stay for as long as you like," Wren said, her eyes twinkling again. "In fact, I'd be delighted."

"I'm just considering it," Ari said quickly. "I haven't decided anything."

Wren's hidden smile was quickly turning into a hidden laugh, but fortunately Teddy claimed her attention at that moment, and Ari was given time to gather his thoughts.

"It is nice here," he commented, when Wren was once again free to speak to him. "So much more relaxed than our castle at home, isn't it?" He shook his head in amazement. "Violet's taken me to the beach more than once without anyone following—not a maid, not even a guard! Can you imagine being allowed to actually leave the castle without a guard when you were a Mistran princess?"

Wren scrunched up her nose. "It would definitely never

have happened, but truth be told it shouldn't really happen here either. Inside the castle is fine, but none of the princesses should really be leaving the city itself unguarded." She sighed. "To be perfectly honest, our royal guard is stretched very thin. With so many princesses, it was always a bit of a challenge. Now there's also a queen and king as well as the dowager queen. And more to the point, we have Teddy and Azure."

She glanced at the half dozen guards standing a stone's throw away, out of earshot of their conversation but alert and watchful. "They're certainly the best guarded children in Entolia. In any event, the best solution we could find was to ease off the guard presence required for those of Basil's sisters who are of age. Since Lilac almost always stays with her mother, that only really leaves Violet traipsing about unsupervised. Although Daisy isn't far off turning eighteen."

Ari nodded absently, uninterested in Lilac's habits or Daisy's age. "From what I've seen, Violet doesn't use her freedom to get up to anything Basil would disapprove of," he said. He rubbed the blade of grass between his fingers again. "I saw her on the way here, actually. She was meeting with someone I didn't recognize. A young man. Do you know who it was?"

Wren was once again hiding a smile—not very successfully —but she narrowed her eyes in thought. "A young man—oh, I suppose that was Yannick. I heard he was coming to the castle today."

"Who's Yannick?" Ari asked, a little too quickly.

"He's the son of Ulrich, the wealthiest merchant in Tola, who also happens to be the head of the Merchants' Guild. Yannick will inherit an incredibly wealthy and influential empire one day." She bit her lip, looking worried.

"What is it?" Ari prompted, uneasy. "What's wrong? Should Violet not be meeting with him?"

"No, she should," said Wren quickly. "She's been liaising with the Merchants' Guild on Basil's behalf. Basil's encouraged her from the start to negotiate directly with Yannick where possible. He's always optimistic that those of the younger generation will deal better together."

She met his eye seriously. "Between you and me, it's quite a mess. We're all very concerned. It's the alliance that's the cause of contention. There have been complaints ever since the war ended and Basil allowed Mistran merchants to trade within Entolia again. But it's only under Ulrich's influence that things have reached such a crisis. The merchants' demands are unreasonable, but they're refusing to budge. They're even starting to mutter about a guild-wide trade embargo on the city of Tola."

Ari gave a low whistle.

"I didn't know there was still so much tension," he said. He frowned. "And I had no idea Violet was in the middle of such a stressful situation. Is that what's been making her uncomfortable?" He felt both foolish and guilty for his trickle of disappointment. Likely her melancholy had nothing to do with him leaving at all.

"Uncomfortable?" Wren asked. "What do you mean?"

Ari shrugged. "I've noticed it a few times. And I noticed it again when I saw her speaking with this Yannick."

Wren frowned, but whatever she was about to say was lost as Azure made a dive for the water's edge, almost succeeding in catapulting herself out of her mother's arms.

"Zuzu, no!" Wren said. "Stop that. No, don't put it in your mouth." She gently but firmly removed a ball from the one-year-old's hand. Ari hadn't even noticed her playing with it.

The toddler fought her mother for custody of the ball, yelling at the top of her considerable voice as she tried again to wriggle free.

"Tiss! Tiss!"

A nursemaid hurried forward, apparently having been hovering back with the guards. She offered to take the screaming child from the queen, but Wren waved her off with a word of thanks.

"You're all right, Zuzu," said Ari soothingly. "Want to come sit on Uncle Ari's lap for a while?"

"You can try, but at your own peril," Wren told him dryly. She handed Azure over, and Ari took a firm hold of the toddler, conscious of the pond close by. It looked deep.

"There we go," he said cheerfully, but the small child wasn't listening. She was still shouting *tiss*—whatever that meant—as loudly as she could and reaching out her little fists to reclaim the ball. She wasn't coordinated enough to grab it from her mother, however. All she succeeded in doing was to knock it from Wren's hands. It fell to the ground, rolling promptly toward the pond, where it disappeared into the water.

Azure instantly set up a wail, diving toward the pond. Ari kept her in a secure grip, but he didn't blame Wren for her evident alarm.

"Let me take her," his sister said, reclaiming her child. "I'm sorry, Zuzu, but the ball is gone. It'll be at the bottom of the pond by now."

"Time for Uncle Ari to come to the rescue," Ari declared, standing up and stripping off his jacket.

"Ari, you don't need to—"

Ari didn't wait for Wren to finish, striding straight forward into the pond. It was cold, and slanted downward more quickly than he expected. He'd hoped to just feel around for the ball, but it quickly became clear that wouldn't do it. Taking a deep breath, he dove into the water, his eyes searching the murkiness for a glint of gold. His first attempt yielded nothing, but after resurfacing for a breath, he tried again with more success. The ball was nestled at the bottom in a patch of waterweeds.

Ari dove down, thinking humorously how much easier it had been to dive through water when he was a swan. His movement startled a frog which was sitting on the bottom, just near the golden ball, and the creature glided away from Ari's questing hand.

When Ari emerged from the water, he was given a hero's welcome by Azure, who wasted no time in snatching the ball from him and trying again to put it in her mouth. When she pulled away from the water, Wren let her down, and she began to toddle toward her brother, who was playing happily in the dirt nearby.

The three-year-old looked up with interest at her approach, and inevitably questioned his sister's right to sole custody of the ball. The resultant tussle caused Wren to confiscate the ball, which she handed absently to Ari while she restored peace between her children.

Ari threw it from one hand to the other, admiring its shine. "No wonder she dropped it," he commented, when Wren at last rejoined him. "Why is it so heavy?"

"Because, as best I can tell, it's made of solid gold," Wren said. She rolled her eyes. "Next time I write to Mother and Father, I'll have to ask them why in the world they would think a pair of toddlers—royal or otherwise—need solid gold toys to play with."

"Mother and Father?" Ari asked, surprised. "This is from our parents?"

Wren nodded. "It was an official gift from the delegation."

Ari frowned in confusion. He had no memory of his parents sending a gift for Wren's children. And it wasn't an official delegation, he'd seen to that. Before he could ask Wren about it, Azure barreled up to them, flinging her arms around her mother's legs and complaining incomprehensibly about some disaster. Taking advantage of Wren's distraction, Ari slipped the ball into the pocket of his jacket, which was slung over his arm.

He couldn't explain why, but he felt uneasy about the golden ball. He wanted to find out where exactly it came from before returning it to his niece and nephew.

But investigating their toy would have to wait. For the moment, he was sopping wet and needed to get into dry clothes before he was expected for dinner. He took his leave of Wren, hurrying back into the castle.

Lex, who was waiting for him in his rooms, tutted at the sight of his dripping form and hastened to select fresh clothes for the evening meal. Back in Mistra, Lex didn't act as a personal servant for any of the royals, but he'd been filling the role since their arrival in Tola. Ari didn't mind. He liked having someone familiar around him, rather than relying on Entolian servants who were all total strangers.

"Tonight is a farewell dinner of sorts, is it not, Your Highness?" Lex asked, as he helped Ari don his dry garments.

"I think so, but it's nothing official," Ari said, still mulling on the question of whether he would really leave in the morning as intended.

"If I may, Your Highness," Lex said deferentially, "I wished to speak to you about your onward journey."

"Of course," said Ari. "What is it?"

The servant cleared his throat. "Well, I wondered if you might give me leave to return to Myst rather than continuing with you. I have no doubt the other servants in our group are more than capable of seeing to your needs."

Ari regarded the older man in surprise. He hadn't guessed that Lex was having doubts about the trip to Bansford—after all, the servant had volunteered to come with him in the first place. Perhaps he'd found the time in Entolia more taxing than expected, and wished for the familiar comfort of home. It wasn't Ari's tendency, but he didn't blame the servant for being different from him.

"Of course, Lex," he said. "You'll be missed, but I'm very willing to release you."

"Thank you, Your Highness," said Lex, bowing his head.

Ari nodded absently, his eyes on his reflection as he straightened his tunic. The evening was warm, so he draped his jacket over his arm rather than wearing it. He might want it later.

He turned from the looking glass with renewed energy, eager to be gone. After all, whatever other commitments she'd had during the afternoon, Violet would surely be present at dinner.

# CHAPTER FIVE

## Violet

Violet tried not to fidget as Yannick consulted his notes yet again.

"My father also wished me to inquire about the issue of access to the Entolian ambassador for those members of our Merchants' Guild operating in Mistra at present."

"Yannick." Violet cut him off, leaning forward on her elbows. She'd been very patient through the last two hours of these types of requests, but she'd reached her limit. "I have no new information on any of that, and no authority to unilaterally make changes, as you must surely know. To speak plainly, I thought the purpose of our meeting today was to discuss my proposal. Do we have a deal or not?"

Yannick sat back, steepling his fingers as he considered her. "I appreciate your desire for an immediate answer. But we still have matters to consider."

"We?" Violet repeated, raising an eyebrow.

Yannick gave a thin smile. "All right, I. My father is very much in favor of the idea. But I acknowledge I've been less certain. I mean no offense, but after all, it's no small matter to sign away one's life."

"True." Violet inclined her head in acknowledgment. "I'm not offended. But I do want an answer."

Yannick nodded slowly. "Forgive the bluntness of the question, but how old are you, Princess Violet?"

Violet was taken aback, but on reflection she supposed it was a reasonable question. "I'm nineteen."

"Hmm." Yannick rubbed his palms together slowly. "I'm twenty-five. You are, perhaps, a little young for me."

Violet frowned. She didn't see the difference in their ages as substantial.

"You have one older unmarried sister, I believe," Yannick prompted delicately. "Would Princess Lilac be a more appropriate choice, perhaps?"

"It doesn't matter whether she's more appropriate, she's not the deal that's being offered," said Violet shortly.

She couldn't help but feel irked. Perhaps he preferred Lilac in appearance—while neither sister was considered unattractive, they did have different styles—but it felt a bit impudent for him to suggest a cold trade.

In any event, it was out of the question. No thought of sacrificing one of her sisters had ever crossed Violet's mind in her scheming. As annoying as Lilac could be at times, Violet wasn't about to push her into a political marriage merely for the crime of being two years older than Violet was.

"If you don't wish to form this alliance, Yannick, I will understand perfectly," Violet added steadily. "And I will take no offense. But that will be the end of the matter. I wasn't offering an open account for you to choose whichever princess you want as a bride."

"I understand," said Yannick, raising his hands in defense. "I meant no offense, as I said." He studied her face again. "I do wish for an amicable resolution to our current conflict, as you clearly do as well. I can see the merit in your suggestion, and

I'm inclined to think we could make it work. But..." He hesitated. "But I do have some questions."

"Ask away," Violet said promptly.

"Would our union take place soon?"

"If you wish," said Violet.

Yannick nodded. "Would you be required to renounce your title, or in some other way lose your privileges due to marrying someone outside the nobility?"

Violet frowned at him. She would be grateful for his thoughtfulness if she knew him well enough to be sure the question was asked out of consideration for her situation. It could just as easily be concern over his own status.

"Of course not," she said. "You wouldn't become a prince or anything. But I would keep my title as a princess, and my position in the royal family. If you wanted it, my brother would probably grant you an honorary title of some sort. It would be just like when my eldest sister Zinnia married Obsidian. He isn't part of the nobility, you know." Not that Obsidian had accepted a title, being uninterested in his own consequence. But she didn't say that.

Yannick smiled in amusement. "Not a true comparison, Your Highness. The fact that he isn't a nobleman is insignificant in light of his status as a powerful enchanter. Would we need to live in our own dwelling, separate from the castle, then, as they do?"

Violet shrugged. "Not necessarily. That was merely their preference. We could live in the castle if you wish."

"I would wish that," Yannick said. "In fact," he squared his shoulders, "I would be grateful for the opportunity to sojourn in the castle now, to better understand the life to which I would be committing myself. Although of course I realize I would be merely a guest at this stage," he added quickly.

Violet narrowed her eyes. Again, she found the request

impudent, however politely it was worded. He wished to try it out before committing himself, did he? Probably wanted his influence pandered to while the dispute was still ongoing, and Basil still needed to step carefully around the Merchants' Guild. She told herself to swallow her annoyance—it was no news to her that this whole conflict was really about ego. But she couldn't quite bring herself to just bow to his requests.

"You want guarantees, Yannick," she said bluntly. "So I'm sure you understand me wanting the same. Is the purpose of our proposed union fully understood?"

"Of course," he assured her. "You have my word of honor that if our marriage goes ahead, my father will stop all protests regarding the Mistran merchants. And the rest of the guild will follow him."

Violet nodded slowly. She still wasn't entirely sure what she thought about his request, and she reminded herself that she was a princess in her own castle, and needn't let herself be pressured into a hasty answer.

"Then I see no barrier to our union proceeding," she said, rising to her feet. "But I suggest we leave the matter for now, and I will consider your request regarding accommodation in the castle. We can meet again in a few days' time."

She thought Yannick looked a little disappointed that she hadn't acquiesced at once, but he hastened to stand as well, dipping into a bow.

"As you wish, Your Highness. I will await your contact."

With a final nod, Violet swept from the room. The conversation had gone so long, she would need to hurry to get to dinner on time. And she couldn't be late. Not when it was Ari's last night.

The thought made her heart sink, the reaction much stronger than it should have been. All week she'd been trying to deny her growing dread over his departure. She'd thrown herself into their activities—into his company—with enthusiasm, trying not to give her mind time to think about what would happen when he left. The Mistran prince's departure had become inextricably linked in her mind with the progression of her plans with Yannick.

Next week she might embark on a loveless political union, possibly never seeing Ari again. *This* week, she would enjoy every minute—both of being free and of being in the company of someone who made her feel so alive. What did she have to lose, after all?

But the closer they came to Ari leaving, the more it was brought home to her that she did have something to lose, something which his company had peeled away alarmingly quickly: her peace of mind. Before Ari had arrived, she'd regarded her planned political alliance not with pleasure, but with a sort of unemotional resignation. Now, for some reason, it was almost unbearable to contemplate it.

So she didn't contemplate it. She just kept going with her plans, giving them as little thought as possible while she focused all her mind and energy on her time with Ari.

When she entered the dining hall, however, and saw Ari chatting animatedly to Wren, the pang that went through her told her that she hadn't succeeded in separating her emotions as much as she'd thought. He seemed in fairly good spirits, his ready laugh ringing across the space between them. The contrast of the two siblings was striking—Wren's quiet grace accentuating the suppressed energy that always radiated from Ari. Some might find it overwhelming, or even immature. But Violet didn't feel that way. He was someone who enjoyed life, and that called to her irresistibly.

She remembered thinking, the morning after he arrived, that it would be inconvenient timing for her to find someone attractive, especially someone she could so conceivably form a union with. She couldn't imagine either royal family protesting at another marriage to strengthen the alliance.

But her thoughts were running away with her to be contemplating marriage. Could that memory really be only a week earlier? It felt much longer. And in the week they'd spent together, she'd come to know Ari a hundred times better than she knew Yannick, with whom she was likely about to embark on a lifelong commitment.

Quite suddenly, Ari looked up, his eyes finding her by the door and a bright smile of welcome crossing his face. Violet returned the smile as naturally as she could, her heart twisting as she crossed the room to sit beside him.

Could she really go through with her bloodless plans with Yannick? Would she be wrong to do so, if she could feel this way merely from Ari smiling at her? Maybe an unemotional union wasn't for her—maybe attraction wasn't so bad after all. She'd thought the timing inconvenient, but what if it was actually perfectly timed in order to save her from herself? What if she and Ari were *meant* to be together, and he'd showed up just in time to prevent her from making an irrevocable mistake?

It sounded fanciful even in her head, but after all, such things did happen. Both her brother and her eldest sister had found a love every bit as romantic and sincere as her imaginings. She'd never experienced it herself, which was why she'd thought very little of serving her kingdom through an unemotional political union. But now, with Ari, she was starting to think it had found her at last. And judging by the warmth of his gaze as she sank into a chair beside him, it didn't seem impossible that he might be feeling the same.

"Ari," she greeted him. "You've gone up in the world, sitting beside the queen."

He grinned at her. "You joke, but it would be true if we were in my family's castle. We don't sit all over the place as we please like you do. It's a very rigid process, and everyone has their assigned place."

Violet laughed. "Yes, Wren's told us that we're shockingly informal. It's just too hard to keep order with so many of us."

Basil arrived as she spoke, and the meal began. Violet leaned around Ari and Wren to direct a question at her brother.

"Is this everyone? Aren't Zinnia and Obsidian coming for Ari's farewell dinner?"

Basil frowned in an effort of memory. "I don't think so. How did your meeting with Yannick go, by the way?"

"Well enough," said Violet lightly. She caught Ari watching her thoughtfully, and hastened to dig into her food.

"I think Zinnia is planning to come for breakfast to see you off, Ari," Wren said. "She was going to stay on so that Genny could play with her cousins for a while." She named Zinnia and Obsidian's two-year-old daughter.

"Shame," said Violet. "I was hoping Obsidian would be here so I could ask him to help with my necklace." Wren looked confused, so she added, "The one trapped down the side of the bureau. I thought he might be able to get it out with magic."

"Your necklace," said Basil apologetically. "I forgot again."

"Don't worry about it." Violet waved a hand. "It's not important, honestly. I'll catch Obsidian another time."

"Is it a valuable necklace?" Ari asked, claiming her attention from her other side as someone else called to Wren and Basil.

"Not really," Violet said with a shrug. "Just sentimental. Zinnia gave it to me when we were children, and it's always been my favorite."

The meal drew on, Ari full of cheerful chatter. Occasionally someone else directed a question to him, often about his onward journey, or asked Violet a question. But each time, his attention returned immediately to her. She was conscious the whole time of having his full focus. Having grown up in a large and chaotic family, one plagued by illness, war, and magical curses, Violet didn't have much experience with the sensation.

She enjoyed it immensely.

In fact, the more minutes ticked by, the less she could think about anything but Ari. He couldn't leave in the morning. She couldn't go back to the way things were before. Her life had seemed fine before Ari arrived, but now it looked bleak in memory. And that was without even considering the question of marriage with Yannick. That image was...unthinkable.

"So how will you travel?" someone asked Ari, pulling his gaze from her face. "By horse?"

"Actually," said Ari, his eyes straying back to Violet, "I've been rethinking that."

Violet's eyes flew to his. What was he saying? Was he truly rethinking leaving? On the other side of the table, one of the younger girls dropped a dish, and Ari's answer got lost in the kerfuffle. But Violet found herself unable to take her eyes off his face.

A sudden boldness rushed over her, and she put her fork down.

"Ari," she said, her voice steady. "Would you like to join me for some fresh air?"

Ari stood at once, offering her his arm. Disregarding what anyone else might be thinking of their actions, Violet took it. She glanced at the double doors onto the patio they'd escaped to on Ari's first night in Tola. The doors were closed, and she could see through the glass that the weather had turned since the afternoon. Rain was pattering down. But that didn't trouble her.

"Bring your jacket," she told Ari softly. "You might want it outside."

She pulled her own shawl tightly around her shoulders as she led the way to the double doors. She heard her mother start to say something, but Basil cut her off cheerfully, likely prompted by Wren. Violet had often noticed her sister-in-law's eyes on the pair when they were all together. But she couldn't even find it in herself to be embarrassed by whatever understanding they thought she and Ari might have. Who knew, maybe they'd be right by the end of the evening?

Without a word, she slipped out through the doors and into the night, conscious of Ari behind her as she crossed the patio. A decorative wall stretched across the platform's edge before giving way to a shallow staircase into the gardens beyond, and Violet leaned against the wall, listening to the sound of the rain. She felt Ari approach, but he hovered behind her, not joining her at the railing.

"Is everything all right, Violet?" His voice was soft.

Gathering her courage, Violet turned. "Not really," she acknowledged. "I've been struggling for a while now."

Ari frowned, moving forward at last and draping his jacket over the edge of the wall before leaning on it with his elbows. "Is it about the conflict with the Merchants' Guild? Wren told me about it. I saw you with that merchant's son earlier, and you looked uncomfortable, like you do from time to time."

Violet stared at him. He'd seen her with Yannick? He'd seen her discomfort at other times? He must be the only one.

"You noticed that?" she asked faintly, struggling to marshal her thoughts.

"Of course," said Ari. His brow creased in concern. "It was the same as how you seemed earlier, when Basil asked you about the meeting. Did something happen?"

Violet shook her head, a lump rising in her throat.

"Never mind about all that. That's not what I was going to say." Her courage failing her, she gazed out at the rain-spattered garden instead of at Ari's face. "I'm struggling because of you. I've enjoyed your visit so much. Too much, I think."

Ari was silent for so long that she snuck a look at him. His eyes were on her, and his expression made her breath catch a little.

"I've enjoyed it, too," he said. "Much more than I expected to. You...you're like no one I've ever met before, Violet."

Violet felt her face warm with pleasure. "I'm not that extraordinary."

"Yes you are," said Ari simply. "Or you are to me, anyway. No one else has ever made me feel quite like I do when I'm in your company." He sent her a swift grin. "You certainly keep me guessing, anyway."

Violet laughed. "Life would be boring without a little unpredictability."

"Agreed," said Ari, laughing as well.

A gust of wind passed over them, and he paused to don his jacket. Slipping his hands into his pockets, he fidgeted for a moment. Violet had the impression he was stalling.

"If you've enjoyed my visit," he said at last, "why would that be a struggle? Is it...is it because I'm leaving tomorrow? Because if I'm honest, I've struggled with that as well."

An eager hope rushed over Violet, and she turned to face him at last. "What if you weren't leaving tomorrow, though? What if I asked you to stay?"

Ari's breath hitched audibly, and he shifted closer. "Honestly, Violet, I don't think there's anything you could ask me that I'd find easy to refuse." He reached one hand toward her, his fingers strong as they brushed her cheek. "I've never met anyone I've wanted so much to say yes to." He smiled, the expression softer than his usual exuberant grin. "No matter how outrageous your ideas can be."

Violet tried to smile at his banter, but her thoughts were in too much disarray. Butterflies rioted in her stomach at his touch, and every nerve felt alive from his proximity, from his words. Closing her eyes, she leaned toward him, fully consumed by the moment. She couldn't go through with her proposal to Yannick, not when she felt this way about Ari. It was simply impossible. If Ari was willing to stay in Tola for her, she was willing to fight for him. They would have to find another way through the conflict with the Merchants' Guild.

"Violet," Ari said, his voice soft in her ears. "I left home because I was restless. Not just a little bit restless, but unbearably so. I wanted adventure, which is why the idea of crossing the desert appealed so much to me. But maybe I was wrong about the kind of adventure I was looking for. I've been struggling these last few days, too. I've been wondering if maybe I should be embracing what's before me rather than chasing something unknown."

Violet opened her eyes, his words encouraging her to hope. Ari was so close, it was hard to breathe. One hand was still fidgeting in the pocket of his jacket, belying the poised front he was trying to convey. His other hand lifted again, brushing some hair back off her shoulder. She'd thought he was going to say more, but he remained silent, so she cleared her own throat.

"I don't know if I get a vote, but personally I think that sounds like a fantastic idea," she said hopefully. She swallowed, determined to be bold. "Ari, I want you to stay."

She gave him her most winning smile, willing him to raise his eyes to her face again. There was no way he could fail to understand her meaning. Nerves fluttered pleasurably over her. Would he speak as plainly? Would he kiss her? He'd seemed close to it before.

But he didn't seem close now. His hand fell from her hair, and he didn't quite meet her eyes. Violet watched, confused, as he shifted on his feet, as if ill at ease.

"Ari?" she prompted. His eyes slid over her shoulder, and she turned a little, wondering if he was self-conscious at the proximity of her family. Surely he would know that they wouldn't be able to see them out in the darkness.

Of course, the same wasn't true in reverse. With the dining hall so well lit, Ari and Violet could see the scene through the glass doors with ease. The family didn't seem to be looking their way, too focused on their meal. But there was a row of servants standing behind them, and several of them were looking toward the windows. Still, Violet didn't think they could actually see the pair.

"Ari?" she tried again. "What's wrong?"

He still didn't reply, his eyes riveted on the room within. Frowning, Violet followed his gaze, unable to help the irritation that rose in her at his distraction, in this of all moments. One of the things she liked most about him was the intensity of his usual focus.

A feeling of unease spread over her as she looked between Ari and the group inside. She wasn't usually prone to petty jealousy, but she couldn't help but notice that his eyes seemed to be fixed on the row of servants, more than one of whom were attractive young women, including some who waited on Violet from time to time. Was it possible—a horrible, embarrassing thought—that she'd misinterpreted what or whom he wished to "embrace" in this different type of adventure?

She cleared her throat. "It seems I'm capable of being boring after all," she told him, not even caring that she sounded snarky. "I guess I need to keep you guessing a bit more."

"What?" Ari brought his gaze back to her, his expression confused. "I'm sorry, Violet, what were you saying?"

She frowned as she searched his face. "Are you all right?" she asked. "You were acting strange."

"Was I?" he asked, grimacing. "I'm sorry, I guess I'm nervous."

Violet softened. "I can understand that," she said. "It's not a small decision, upending your plans. But...do you really think you might stay?"

Ari didn't respond. His eyes had been on her face as she spoke, but as soon as she'd posed her question, they slid past her, once again settling on someone or something inside the dining hall.

"Ari," she said, not trying to disguise her impatience this time.

"I'm sorry," he said again, his eyes flicking back to her. "Violet, I'm really sorry. I...there's more I want to say, but I...can't. I have to go. I'm very sorry, but I have to go."

Violet's mouth fell open, confusion warring with embarrassment. "Oh," she said. "I, uh, I understand. I didn't mean to push you into—"

"I have to go, Violet," said Ari, cutting her off. "I'm sorry."

And before she could blink, he'd hurried past her and was pushing his way through the double doors. Violet stared after him, barely taking in the bustle within the room as the meal broke up and servants began clearing plates from the table. Cold rushed in to take the place of Ari's warm presence, and she felt more humiliated than she ever had in her life. She stood there for several long minutes, trying to get her head around the abrupt change. What had come over Ari? She'd never seen him behave that way. Had she pushed too hard?

Unable to face any of her family, Violet re-entered the dining room with a quick stride, hurrying into the corridor and toward her own suite. Only once she was alone and away from prying eyes did she let her emotions show. What a fool she'd been! How embarrassing that she'd thought Ari would melt in her hand, throw away all his plans for her.

But the memory of his warm smile as he told her she was like no one he'd ever met before intruded on her miserable thoughts. She hadn't imagined the connection between them.

She had no idea why he'd behaved so strangely, but she told herself not to make a hasty judgment. Perhaps she'd been a little too forward and spooked him. It wasn't so difficult to understand.

Violet gave a curt nod into the darkness of her room. She was too sensible to be so easily overset. There was nothing she could do about her current mortification, but she could avoid letting it push her to take drastic action. There wasn't much time left before his departure, but there was still some. She would give them both the night to clear their heads, and speak to him properly in the morning.

# CHAPTER SIX

## *Ari*

Ari walked into the dining hall, his mind in a fog. He was confused, different sensations pulling him in different directions. Part of his mind was aware that he'd left his conversation with Violet very unfinished. He was even aware—very faintly—of the tingling excitement he'd felt at her words. She'd been so near.

And yet, he couldn't properly recapture either what she'd said or how he'd felt. His mind was caught by another priority, one he simply couldn't deny. It was like a compulsion, drawing him back into the room. He followed it almost blindly, struggling to comprehend his own movements. He didn't know why he was re-entering the building, just that he needed to do it.

The rest of the family had finished eating, and most had risen from the table. Servants moved about the space, some clearing food while others accompanied the younger princesses toward the door, ready to assist them in their nightly preparations. Hardly aware of where he was going, Ari found himself leaving the room as well. No one took particular notice of him in the general bustle, and he was surprised to find himself heading not toward his suite, but toward the castle's eastern exit, the one that led to the cliffs and the hills beyond.

He wasn't conscious of specifically following someone, but a couple of times, when turning a corner, Ari thought he caught a glimpse of a figure ahead. As he traversed the corridors, his mind fought against itself, half of it wanting to return to Violet, the other half determined to go on. He was unsettled, his stride choppy and his hands fidgeting as he tried to reclaim control of himself.

It wasn't until he'd actually left the courtyard and found himself on the windswept hilltop that he managed to bring himself fully to a stop.

"What am I doing?" he muttered, squinting in the rain that was still falling. "Why am I following this compulsion?"

Saying the words aloud helped him to recognize it for what it was. It was a compulsion, and an unnatural one. He'd never experienced anything like it before, but it must be magical in nature. Nothing else made sense. Even knowing that, he was still desperate to continue, and it took all his willpower not to obey.

His hand shifted in his pocket, and suddenly he became aware that his hand was *in* his pocket. But the pocket wasn't empty. There was something in there, something that he'd been fidgeting with since he was on the patio, when he was working up the nerve to tell Violet how he felt. He'd been utterly unaware of the object, but his fingers were wrapped around—

Ari drew the golden ball from its hiding place, staring at it in alarm. He'd known from the start that something was off about the item. Formal his parents might be, but they weren't ridiculous enough to think that royal children needed solid gold toys. Who had sent this item, and with what purpose?

Knowing there was magic in it made it a hundred times more sinister.

Ari realized all at once that his feet were moving again. He forced himself to a stop, slipping the ball back into his pocket and yanking his hand free as his eyes searched the darkness. He'd thought he saw a figure ahead of him in the castle earlier. Who was it? Had they somehow used the ball to compel him?

He glanced behind him, hesitating. Wren needed to be warned about the artifact, but the warning would be much more useful if he could identify who was behind it. Perhaps he should go on, see if he could catch a glimpse of the culprit while he had the chance. His gaze latched on to a shape moving in the darkness ahead, and he crept forward slowly, hoping to avoid detection.

Mercifully, the rain was beginning to slacken, and the gathering darkness was on his side as he edged around the city wall, his eyes fixed on the person ahead. It was a slight form, from what he could see. He could probably best them in a fight if it came to that. But he'd still do well to proceed with caution, especially if magic was involved.

As he approached, he heard voices that caused him to slow his steps still further. It appeared the figure had joined a larger group. The speakers weren't murmuring stealthily, as he would expect. Their voices were loud, almost raucous.

"There you are!" one called, as the person Ari was following merged with the group. From what he could make out in the gloom, they were all very young. "Took you long enough."

The newcomer grunted. "Why should I be in a hurry to waste my time?"

A tutting sound greeted the words. "Don't let Master Enchanter Hughes hear you calling his coursework a waste of time!"

"I'm telling you," the new arrival said, in a stubborn tone that suggested he'd told them the same many times already, "this isn't a real assignment. Turn one creature into another? That's absurd. Not one of us has the power or the finesse to do that. I don't know if any enchanter in Solstice could do it. You certainly can't."

"We'll see about that," said another young man, the grin clear in his voice even though Ari couldn't make out his face.

Ari frowned to himself, hovering back against the city wall. By his best guess, the group was made up of young enchanters and enchantresses, most likely students of Entolia's Enchanters' Guild. They might have the resources to create an artifact like the golden ball. But what could be their motive? And it wasn't as though they were trying to hide. Perhaps their presence here had nothing to do with it. He glanced around, frustrated. If that was so, he'd well and truly lost his real lead by now.

"It is real," another insisted in response to the newcomer's words. "I heard Master Enchanter Hughes give him the assignment myself."

"So did I," said the skeptic impatiently. "But that doesn't mean it was real. You heard how cocky this fool was being, boasting about his natural strength."

"It's not boasting if it's true," said the grinning one.

Ari could almost hear the other student roll his eyes. "Master Enchanter Hughes intentionally set you an impossible task to teach you a lesson. I don't know why we all have to be here to watch you fail. I have better things to do."

"You're not here just to watch," said the other one reassuringly. "You have a central role. You're my subject."

The other student snorted. "You honestly think you have enough power to turn a *human* into some other type of creature? You're delusional. Do you know how much power that would take? Much more than you have."

Ari grimaced, caught up in the drama in spite of himself. He knew from experience that it could be done, but he was inclined to think the student was right. There was no way one untrained young enchanter could do it.

"Ah, but I have more resources than just my innate magic, as strong as it naturally is," said the cocky one maddeningly. "I have my friends."

A chuckle went around the group, and the skeptical one sighed.

"What does that mean?"

"We're going to combine our power," another student explained excitedly. "We think it might be possible with all of our magic working together."

"But we haven't been trained in combining power," protested the first one. "That's supposed to be really complex."

"How hard can it be?" said the cocky student dismissively. Ari strained his eyes in the darkness, trying to catch a glimpse of his face. He seemed to be rolling up his sleeves. "I've given it some thought, and I think it would take a lot of power to try to control the form you'd take. A general enchantment will be more feasible. So we'll turn you into the last animal you've seen."

"This is nonsense," said the target student, sounding unimpressed.

"We need to decide on a counterforce," interjected another one. "If we don't work in a specific way of breaking the enchantment, we'll leave it open to an unintended natural counterforce, which will be much harder to identify and therefore access."

"Yes, thank you for the basic lesson in magic theory," said another student sarcastically.

"He's right, though," the ringleader said fairly. "We do need a counterforce. Any suggestions?"

"How about the enchantment is broken if I punch you in the face?" the subject student deadpanned.

The cocky one chuckled. "Nice try, but most animals can't punch." Ari could hear the grin enter his voice. "How about you have to get a girl to kiss you? That should be next to impossible for you."

"Very funny," said the student, clearly irate.

"I know," piped up a feminine voice, giggling. "He has to be kissed by a *princess* to break the enchantment. That's traditional, right? And it shouldn't be too hard. This kingdom has *twelve* princesses."

"Now you're just being ridiculous," said the odd one out, sounding angrier by the second. "Enough of this nonsense."

"Yes, he's quite right," agreed the ringleader sagely. "Enough joking around. That's an excellent counterforce, I'll work it in. As we discussed, everyone. NOW!"

A chorus of voices rose in a sudden swell, startling Ari.

The target of the enchantment was clearly startled as well. Evidently he hadn't expected them to be ready to act so decisively and with such coordination. With a cry, he jumped aside, dropping to his belly on the grass. Not being an enchanter himself, Ari couldn't sense magic, but he could have sworn he heard the whoosh of the attempted enchantment swooping over the downed student.

Too late he realized his position against the wall put the target of the enchantment directly between him and the group of students. And although the darkness might hide Ari from their eyes, it was no barrier to magic.

With a sudden, overwhelming barrage of sensations, the combined magic slammed straight into Ari.

He keeled over, clutching at his chest in silent terror, but he didn't fall to the ground. Somehow, bizarrely, he was already *on* the ground. He couldn't make sense of his body's position—it was the least of his concerns. His mind was utterly caught in a maelstrom of feelings which could only be described as pure chaos. It was horribly reminiscent of when he'd been turned into a swan, but more haphazard, somehow. It wasn't exactly pain so much as...directionless pandemonium.

When the sensations settled, Ari realized that his hands were pressed against the grass, his face not far above them. But the feel of it was all wrong. Everything was all wrong. He tried to crawl—crawl? stumble? he couldn't tell—forward, but the movement was so jerky, he stopped at once, his head spinning dizzily. He had to fight the urge to be sick. What had happened? What had that uncontrolled jumble of juvenile magic done to him?

Fearfully, Ari lifted his hand in front of his eyes to see the damage. He froze in absolute horror at the sight of a small, green appendage, with three gelatinous prongs in place of fingers. Ari brought his head whipping around to look at his feet. Sure enough, they had transformed into the same slimy, green surface, this time with webs connecting them. His tongue unlocked, he released an involuntary scream which came out as a low, painful croak.

He'd been turned into a frog.

He'd been turned into a FROG! No! It couldn't be real. This couldn't be happening. He was having a horrible dream, the type he'd had sometimes in the early days of his return to human form. True, those visions had never involved being cursed into an amphibian form. But it was the only explanation he could accept. He couldn't possibly have survived six years as a swan only to be turned into a pond frog by an accident of a group of untrained students. No one person could be *that* unlucky.

Even as his mind tried to deny it, every surface on Ari's body confirmed the horrifying truth. What had the cocky student said? *We'll turn you into the last animal you've seen.* Ari's terrified, paralyzed mind flew back to the afternoon, when he'd fished little Azure's ball out of the pond in the castle garden. He distinctly remembered the morose-looking frog he'd seen squatting beside it. It was, in fact, exactly the type of frog Ari now resembled.

"Oi! What are you lot doing?" The sharp voice brought Ari's attention to a new arrival to the scene, this one considerably beyond youth. The man strode purposefully through the gloom, a lantern held aloft in one hand. "I was informed you'd all headed up here, and I don't doubt you're up to no good, skulking on the hillside in the darkness. What's the meaning of this?"

"Master Enchanter Hughes!" gasped the student who'd dived out of the way, sounding relieved in spite of his earlier insistence that the feat was impossible. "They tried to curse me! They tried combining their power to turn me into an animal!"

"WHAT?" the enchanter roared.

"But Master Enchanter, those were your instructions!" protested the ringleader. "You said I was to—"

"I know what I said," the enchanter cut him off, sounding furious. "And I think you're perfectly aware I never intended it as a real assignment—it was an impossible task, designed solely to reduce the size of your head. You, young man, need a lesson in humility!"

"I told you so," muttered the intended target of the enchantment.

"Even if you misunderstood my intention," the older man went on, "I certainly never instructed you to try the magic on another *human*! Or to combine your magic with that of multiple other students, when none of you have received any training in combined power." He clucked his tongue. "It's a very good thing you failed to perform the intended enchantment. Who knows what would have happened if you'd actually hit someone with such a hodgepodge mess of power!"

Ari let out a frantic croak, but no one in the group seemed to even hear him.

"Now back inside the city, all of you. Your parents will certainly be hearing of this." He jabbed a finger at the ringleader. "And no more practical assignments for you. You'll be working on theory alone until I deem you responsible enough to be trusted with power!"

He shepherded the students back toward the city gate, deaf to the protests of the bigheaded one. Knowing he was rapidly losing his window for communicating to the group what had happened, Ari tried to race after them. But he was clumsy in his new body, his progress slow and uneven as he moved in lopsided hops. He kept falling over himself, and the humans quickly moved out of his sight. He tried to call after them, but of course all that emerged was a desperate, throaty croak. He was nowhere near catching up to them when they passed through the gate, and it closed behind them with a horribly final bang.

Ari kept hopping, his long back legs sending him flying in strange directions as he progressed painfully toward the city wall. By the time he reached it, there was no one in sight, and his anguished croaks produced no effect at all. Trying not to panic, Ari took stock of his situation.

He was a frog, yes. That was unfortunate. But he still had his right mind. Surely he could find a way to reverse this. Surely he could return to his own form.

His mind raced back over the childish confrontation he'd witnessed. They'd specifically discussed the counterforce, so he knew they'd built in a way to lift the enchantment. They'd said the student it was intended for would have to be kissed by a princess to return to normal.

A kiss from a princess...unbidden but inevitable, Ari's thoughts flew instantly to Violet. Violet was a princess. Violet would kiss him. She'd been ready to kiss him on that patio, he was almost sure of it. And instead of leaning in and closing the distance between them, he'd pulled away, giving in to the compulsion of the golden ball like a weak-minded fool. And this was what came of it!

He had to get inside the castle. He had to find Violet! Giving up on the gate, Ari hopped along the wall, gaining more control over his new form with every leap. Long as his day had been, he didn't feel tired. In fact, he felt more alert than he'd been in a long time. Clearly his body knew that his new form was supposed to be nocturnal, whatever his mind thought about it.

He also found that he had no difficulty seeing the wall before him. His eyes cut through the gloom of the night with precision, putting his human sight to shame. He could even make out the green of the grass under his webbed feet, and the gray of the stone wall around which he moved.

It felt like an eternity, but eventually Ari found himself at another entrance. This one was smaller, more of a door than a gate. Ari leaned back and gazed doubtfully up at it, his eyes bulging in the darkness. His legs felt strong and full of energy, ready to propel him. But he doubted he could jump *that* high.

Returning his head to its previous position a mere inch from the grass, he noted the gap under the door. It looked too small, but some instinct was prompting him to try it. Tentatively, he pushed his head into it, shuddering at the pressure of the enclosed space. It was a strange and rather horrible feeling, but he kept moving, his long back legs propelling him forward as his body squished itself into a gap that should have been too small for it. He could feel his skin stretching, allowing his body to change shape slightly. Fighting his human thoughts, which were screaming at him to retreat, Ari trusted his animal instincts and kept moving forward. His time as a swan had helped him learn the wisdom of leaning into instincts rather than human habits. He could only be profoundly grateful that he still had access to his human thoughts. With the lack of organization of the enchanters who'd done this to him, he was lucky he wasn't a mindless mess.

With a sucking pop, Ari emerged out the other side of the door. He'd traveled a fair way from the entrance he'd first tried, which would have taken him into the small eastern courtyard. Instead, he found himself in the garden where he'd sat with Wren just hours before.

Ari hopped forward, making for the building with purpose. When he was halfway across the garden, however, level with the very pond in which he'd seen the frog, he slowed. What was his plan? It would be foolish to race straight into the castle now. Everyone would be in bed, including Violet. And she wouldn't be inclined to see him even if she was awake, given how strangely he'd behaved toward her.

It took Ari a moment to realize the absurdity of this thought. Violet probably didn't want to see the real Ari, but she wouldn't react that way to a frog. She'd have no idea the frog was Ari, and she'd treat him like she would any common frog. Which was to say, she'd probably shoo him out at best or squish him on the spot at worst. As would any other human he tried to hassle in the middle of the night.

Reluctantly, Ari concluded that it made no sense to barge into the castle in his current situation. He would be wiser to take some time to come up with a plan, and to approach in daylight, when everyone was awake and thinking clearly.

Left with few options, he allowed his instincts to once again take over, following the prompting to head toward the pond. As he settled in for what was sure to be a miserable night, he struggled not to give in to despair.

How had he gotten into this mess? He'd thought his previous curse was bad enough. But being a frog was even worse than being a swan.

# CHAPTER SEVEN

## Violet

*The magic tugged at Violet, pulling her forward. Some part of her knew she should resist, but she didn't listen to that voice of gloom. She was willing to go. She was happy to go. One slipper-clad foot stepped in front of the other, the trapdoor coming into sight. Of its own accord, it swung upward, revealing the yawning darkness beyond.*

Violet woke with a gasp, springing up to a sitting position. Her heart was pounding, and her forehead was covered with sweat. She took a moment to re-orient herself in the cool light of dawn.

What had that been about? It had been years since she'd dreamed about the curse. She didn't want her mind to return to that place. She was free now, and so were all her sisters. There was no reason to dwell on it.

She'd woken much earlier than normal, and no one had yet come in to open her curtains, or stoke her fire. Violet slipped from her bed, pulling on a gown at random and running a comb through her disheveled waves. She was fairly certain she wouldn't be able to reclaim sleep, and she wasn't in the mood to lie about in bed.

Once she was respectable, she made her way through the castle, still unsettled by the dream. Or perhaps the dream was only partly responsible. Perhaps embarrassment was as much to be blamed for her unease.

Violet winced as she remembered the scene with Ari the night before. She was still confused about how she could have so badly misread him. He'd really seemed on the point of a declaration. And the next moment he'd all but run away from her. She knew she'd been forward, but he'd never seemed to mind that before.

It was well before the usual breakfast hour, but Violet made her way to the dining hall anyway. She was surprised to find two occupants already within.

"Zinnia!" she cried, hurrying toward her eldest sister. Growing up, she'd always been closer to Zinnia than to any of her other sisters. She missed her now that she lived outside the castle with her family.

"Morning, Violet," said Zinnia, giving her a bleary smile. "You're up early."

"So are you," said Violet. "What are you doing here before breakfast?"

"Genny had me awake before dawn," yawned Zinnia. "And Obsidian had to leave really early as well. Since I was planning to bring Genny along to say goodbye to Prince Ari, I figured we may as well head over with Obsidian and peel off here when he went to the guild."

Violet knelt down next to her two-year-old niece, receiving a hug. "You too full of energy to sleep, Genevieve?" she said.

"Yep!" the toddler cried, bouncing on the balls of her feet. "When's breakfast? I'm hungry!"

Violet chuckled but was saved the necessity of answering as the door opened and a servant entered, bearing the first tray of breakfast fare. Genny raced toward the table, apparently deaf to her mother's cry of warning.

"She'll trip the poor server over," Zinnia muttered.

Violet gave a perfunctory smile. "Obsidian's been at the guild a lot lately," she observed.

Zinnia nodded. "It's a lot more than usual. Apparently the current batch of students has great potential but also a great deal of attitude. Master Enchanter Hughes likes to get Obsidian involved because he says his *war hero and partial royal presence awes them into submission*. His words."

She rolled her eyes, but Violet could tell she didn't really dislike hearing her husband talked up. For her own part, Violet wasn't especially interested in these anecdotes, her mind too full of the incident with Ari. She watched her niece cajoling the servant into moving the food within her reach, realizing too late that her sister's eyes were on her.

"Are you all right, Vi?"

Violet turned to Zinnia with a sigh. "I don't know."

"Sad about Ari leaving?" prompted Zinnia.

"Yes," Violet acknowledged slowly. "But it's more than that. We spoke last night. I...well, I asked him to stay. And at first he seemed to be considering it, but then he got...weird." She could see her sister opening her mouth to speak, so she barreled on before she lost her nerve. "And I dreamed about the curse last night."

"About the curse?" Zinnia stiffened, her hand shifting as if to grab Violet's arm, then dropping back to her side. "Does that happen often?"

Violet shook her head, her eyes on Genny as the little girl raided a platter of steaming bread rolls. "Not for years. It has me all rattled."

"Understandably," Zinnia said, her voice full of sympathy.

Violet regarded her sister thoughtfully. "Do you still dream about it?"

Zinnia sighed. "Sometimes," she admitted.

The answer made Violet sad, but it wasn't surprising. Zinnia had borne the brunt of their curse. The rest of them hadn't even known they were cursed until it was all over. Violet had never felt the compulsion magic that Zinnia had experienced over and over. That was why her dream made no sense.

Gradually, the dining hall filled around them as everyone else arrived for breakfast. Violet tried not to look too eager every time someone entered the room, but she didn't deny to herself that she was watching avidly for Ari. She had no intention of letting the awkward incident the night before pass without discussion. It was unthinkable to let their connection peter out into a vague might-have-been with no closure. One way or another, she and Ari needed to have a frank conversation before he left Tola.

Again and again she was disappointed, as everyone but Ari appeared at the table. She could see that Wren was also confused as to her brother's tardiness, and when the rest of the group were all eating and he was still absent, Violet saw the young queen give a discreet instruction to a serving man. He left the room, only to return a short while later and hurry straight to the queen's side. Surprise and anxiety crossed Wren's face in quick succession, and Violet stood at once.

"What is it?" she asked, when she was close enough for the question to slip under the general hubbub.

Wren's eyes passed from Violet to Basil, their expression one of blank confusion. "Ari's bed hasn't been slept in."

"What?" Violet's mother was obviously sitting close enough to hear, because she swiveled in her chair to face them. "That's peculiar."

"But where is he?" Violet demanded.

Wren shrugged hopelessly. "I don't know. No one seems to."

Violet bit her lip, anxiety creeping over her. Logic told her that Ari could take care of himself. And yet...

"I thought I saw his personal servant this morning," Basil said. "Ari can't be far away. He wouldn't leave without him."

Wren shook her head slowly. "If you mean Lex, Ari actually told me that he'd requested permission to return to Mistra rather than continue on." She frowned. "I assumed Ari would still take the other servants from the group, though. And his guards."

Basil gestured to another servant, who hurried forward. "Check the stables for Prince Ari's horse, please," he said.

"He did say something last night about rethinking his method of transportation, didn't he?" Briar interjected as the servant hurried off. "Maybe he decided to leave his horse and go by some other means. Maybe he wanted more of an adventure and knew that if he waited until morning, everyone would talk him out of it."

Violet swallowed. She remembered the comment. Someone had asked Ari if he'd travel by horse, and he'd said he was rethinking it. She'd assumed he meant he was rethinking the whole trip. Was it possible he truly had been speaking merely about the horse? What a fool she'd made of herself if so!

"Is that the sort of thing he might do?" she asked Wren.

The Mistran ran her thumb over the handle of her spoon in an uneasy motion. "I don't know," she admitted. "He was certainly reckless enough to pull a stunt like that when we were younger. But I thought he'd grown out of that years ago. I thought..." Her eyes flicked to Violet, then to Basil, and she said no more.

"I drove him away," said Violet hollowly.

"Of course you didn't," Wren contradicted quickly, but

Violet shook her head, thinking of the scene on the patio the night before.

"There's more to it than you know. I...I pushed too hard."

It was all she could do not to groan aloud. She'd already been embarrassed. Now she was mortified. She remembered perfectly his unease as he'd told her he needed to go. She hadn't realized he'd meant it so literally, or that he was saying it in response to her request for him to stay in Tola. She'd thought he meant he needed to go somewhere that evening. Perhaps to think it over.

"I can't believe that's true, Violet," Basil said. "He likes you. We've all seen it."

"Likes her?" Zinnia protested. Violet hadn't even heard her approach. "He's smitten! He can't take his eyes off her."

"Let's not do this," said Violet abruptly, unable to bear her entire family witnessing her humiliation. She turned to face her sister, plastering on a tight smile. "He's free to make his own decisions. He was always intending to leave for Bansford this morning. If he decided to go a few hours early, it's no concern of ours. None of us have any claim on him." She met Zinnia's eyes steadily. "Including me."

For an awkward moment, no one said anything. Taking the opportunity while she had it, Violet hurried from the room. Her appetite for breakfast was completely gone. In addition to her embarrassment, she was conscious of concern, and with it, guilt. If Ari had truly run off in this haphazard style, he might be in danger. And she'd caused it by spooking him with her brazenness.

The morning passed painfully, Violet unable to settle to any task. At noon, Wren confirmed to her that there was no sign of Ari, and that no one else from the delegation had left. He'd simply vanished, without any of his things.

"I'm worried, Violet," she said. "It could be that he's run off to Bansford, foolishly deciding to go alone and without supplies for some kind of adventure. But if it's not that, then something's happened to him. How can we know which of those it is?"

"I wish I had the answer," Violet said helplessly. "I'm concerned as well."

Wren moved off, looking distracted, and Violet said no more. She had no doubt her brother would make appropriate inquiries and try to ascertain if there was any evidence of foul play in Ari's disappearance. Most likely someone had already been dispatched up the road that led to Bansford, to try to locate him. But for her part, she didn't place any expectation in those inquiries. She was fairly certain Ari had left by his own choice, and because of her. And if he'd left immediately after their conversation, he had enough of a head start that no messenger would catch up to him for some time.

She drew a shaky breath. There was no sense lamenting what might have been. She'd been hoping for a certain outcome, but evidently Ari's hopes were different. It was absurdly hypocritical of her to complain, after all. She'd already half-formed a betrothal with someone else.

Violet straightened at the thought of Yannick. She knew that Basil was at his wits' end over the merchant crisis. She had a real solution, and she'd let her plans stall because Ari made her heart flutter. In addition to—apparently—being baseless, that had been selfish. It was time to think of the good of the kingdom.

Violet returned to her rooms, summoning a maid to help her make herself more presentable before she joined her family for lunch. She was conscious of being a little disheveled, and she didn't want any pitying looks. She wasn't thrilled when the summons was answered by Naomi, the maid who'd hinted at

Violet's interest in Ari after his first evening with them. But it didn't matter.

While Naomi fussed around selecting a more appropriate gown for the day, Violet pulled a sheet of writing paper toward her. The note she scratched out was short and to the point.

*Dear Yannick*

*Thank you for your patience as I considered your request regarding a stay in the castle. I'm pleased to inform you that your request is acceptable, and I will undertake the appropriate arrangements.*

*Sincerely,*

*Violet*

"Naomi, can you take a message to the courier for me? It's to be delivered to Yannick, the son of the merchant Ulrich. The courier will know where to go."

"Goodness, Your Highness," said the maid, with a titter that grated on Violet's ears. "I suppose it's a princess's right to keep more than one man on the hook."

"Is it?" Violet asked tersely. "You seem to have a strange idea of what princesses' lives are like."

"I'm sure I meant no offense, Your Highness," said Naomi quickly. Violet thought she sounded more sulky than penitent, but perhaps it was her own bitterness speaking. She could rarely remember feeling so bruised.

"It was nice to see little Genevieve at breakfast this morning," said Naomi. "Such a sweet child."

Violet gave a non-committal grunt.

"She and the little prince and princess must be the delight of the family," Naomi pressed, clearly determined to manage some kind of cheerful conversation. "I suppose you often look after your niece and nephew, Your Highness? You must dote on them."

"I'm very fond of them, but I'm not really called upon to watch them," said Violet flatly. "They're overflowing with both aunts and nursemaids. Not to mention their own parents."

"Yes, I've noticed that the queen is more involved with their care than I would expect for a royal family," Naomi commented. "Very admirable, I'm sure," she added quickly, perhaps taking in Violet's expressionless face.

Violet didn't even bother to respond this time, and Naomi seemed to take the hint at last. Giving up on drawing the princess out, the maid dressed Violet's hair in silence. A small part of Violet felt guilty over her rudeness, when the other girl was probably only trying to be friendly. But mostly she was just desperate to be left alone. A couple weeks ago, she'd had no dreams to speak of, and it had seemed a small matter to give her future to the kingdom she loved.

Now that she'd tasted a dream, the prospect was as painful as it was empty. If only Ari hadn't come. If she'd gone on as she was, she'd never have known what it was to feel that kind of hope. And then she'd never have known the crushing despair of watching a dream crumble around her.

# CHAPTER EIGHT

## Ari

Ari woke to the patter of rain on his head. He stretched his leg, confused, and experienced a shock as the limb in question shot out behind him with unnerving force and at an impossible angle.

Oh, that was right. He was a frog.

If frogs could groan, Ari would have let out a powerful one. As it was, he only managed a miserable croak. He opened his eyes—great, bulging organs that they were—and squinted up into the light of the morning. He was sitting on a lily leaf near the edge of the pond. He could vaguely remember succumbing to his exhaustion, in defiance of the instinct that wanted him to be awake during the night.

He couldn't afford to be a nocturnal frog, though. Not if he was going to find a way to communicate with the humans whose help he needed to lift the curse.

Another splat fell on his head, and he realized that it wasn't rain at all. A goose glided across the surface of the water nearby, shaking its wings and splashing Ari in the process. Ari tried to hop off his leaf to the shore, but his ungainly legs sent him jerking in the wrong direction, and the next thing he knew he was adrift, his frantic strokes doing nothing to stop his steady descent to the bottom of the pond.

After a moment he gave up, letting himself drift until he hit the bottom with a soundless thud. His human mind screamed that he needed air, but when he paused to take stock of his frog body, he found that he didn't. No instinct was urging him to hurry to the surface, or to take a breath. He found he was quite satisfied, physically speaking.

Emotionally, he was anything but.

His arrival into the scum that was the floor of the pond prompted a flurry of movement. Following it, Ari saw another frog—bizarrely large to his eyes, given it was the same size as him—taking cover behind some weeds. The creature's eyes bulged with alarm as they rested on the newcomer. It was most likely the very frog he'd seen there the day before. The one that had unknowingly doomed him to his current predicament by being the last animal he saw before he was hit with the patchwork mess of magic released by those students.

*What are you looking at?* Ari thought mutinously. *If I'm ugly, you're ugly.*

Taking a moment to wallow in his misery, Ari looked around him. It was a piteous sight, that much was certain. So far the only benefit he could see to his frog form was that in spite of being fully submerged in a pond, he didn't feel in the least cold.

Small mercies.

Movement above drew his attention, and he looked up to see the goose from earlier coasting across the surface of the water. Its forward movement was smooth, but its webbed feet paddled comically below. Ari felt a pang of nostalgia. He remembered seeing his brothers paddle that way. They'd made fun of each other's awkward gait in the early days. As he watched, the goose flapped its wings, disturbing the water as it took to the sky.

Jealousy cut through Ari. It would be so much better to be that goose, winging its way to freedom from the surface, than a frog stuck at the bottom of the pond.

*No!* he told himself severely. *Stop that.* Had he lost his mind? He didn't want to be a goose. He wanted to be his own human self again! Honestly. He'd never thought he'd see the day when he'd wish he was a waterfowl again.

Steeling himself for an extended journey, Ari pushed himself up with his long back legs. He was an awkward swimmer as a frog, but eventually he managed to reach the edge of the pond. He pulled himself out, having to fight an old, redundant instinct that told him to shake out his wings.

What a mess his mind was. What would he be like when he was a man again? How many magical transformations could a human body sustain before the mind attached to it became permanently addled?

Free of the water, Ari began his tortuous journey toward the castle. Based on the light around him, his best guess was that it was about noon. Clearly his frog instincts had tried to get him to sleep during the day. He would have to be intentional about stopping himself from slipping naturally into a nocturnal sleep cycle.

He'd barely moved away from the water when a shadow loomed suddenly over him. Startled, Ari looked up to see an enormous heron. At least, it looked enormous to a frog. He barely moved in time to dodge its abrupt attack, leaping frantically out of the way of its beak. Fear riding him, he pushed himself forward, his long legs moving with panicked speed as he hopped into a bush. He tried to stay under the cover of the leaves as he lurched unevenly in the direction of the castle. The idea of dying by means of becoming a heron's breakfast was unthinkable.

To his great relief, the heron seemed to lose interest in its fleeing prey as Ari got further from the water. Soon the bird returned to the pond, and he was able to continue more slowly, albeit much more cautiously. His gait was still awkward, and his progress wasn't as quick as he'd like. But no other creatures in the garden took the least notice of him, and it was only once he reached the building that his concern returned. Common sense prodded him to avoid being seen by humans as much as possible, causing him to go even more slowly as he dodged behind plinths and around corners to avoid guards and servants.

He made his way through the corridors, not sure of the best direction to take. When he got his bearings and realized he wasn't far from the dining hall, he decided it was as good a destination as any. With any luck, he'd find Obsidian present this time. Those with magic—enchanters, enchantresses, and dragons—could innately sense its presence. Surely the enchanter would recognize the magic on the intruding frog, even if he didn't know at once what it meant. One way or another, Ari would find a way out of his predicament. Last time, he'd spent six years as a swan. He was determined not to let it be a long-term situation this time. How long did frogs even live?

Ari was just making his uneven way around the last corner before the dining hall when he heard a familiar voice.

"Is my brother already at luncheon?"

*Violet!*

Excitement coursed through him, and he put on an extra burst of speed. Unfortunately his coordination wasn't equal to his energy. His back legs propelled him forward powerfully, but his balance was off, and all he managed to do was to go flying into a suit of armor with a deafening clang.

"What was that?" Violet asked mildly.

Ari peeled himself off one of the metal plates that would protect the shin of anyone wearing the armor. His vision spun as he fell to the floor, trying to get his bearings. The next thing he knew, Violet's face swam into view, as large as a giant's.

"What are you doing here, little fella?" she asked, in much the same voice he'd heard her use on her nieces and nephew.

"Ugh, get back, Your Highness!" shrieked a nearby servant. "It's a frog!"

"Yes, I can see that it's a frog," Violet said, sounding amused. "It won't hurt me, you know."

"But it might have...diseases," protested the maid.

*Very impolite*, Ari thought, sending an amphibian frown toward the servant in question.

"I'll take care of it, Your Highness," said a gruff new voice.

A guard strode forward with purpose, lifting his spear meaningfully so that the butt of it loomed over Ari's head. Alarmed, Ari tried to hop to shelter, but Violet's hand shot out, trapping him.

"Nonsense, there's no need to kill the poor creature! Like I said, it won't do any harm. It must have come in from the garden and gotten lost. All it needs is a ride back to the pond."

"Surely you're not going to carry the creature around, Your Highness!" gasped the maid.

"I surely am," said Violet, unperturbed. With a firm but painless grip, she lifted Ari to shoulder height, taking a good look at him. "You're a very nice-looking frog," she informed him politely. "Very striking yellow stripes. And hardly a wart to be seen."

*Such charming compliments*, Ari thought dryly, for a moment almost forgetting that she couldn't hear his response to her banter. It felt oddly like their usual interactions. He wasn't sure whether to be warmed by how well he'd come to know her, or disheartened by the fact that she seemed to banter that way with everyone.

Even frogs.

"Let me take the frog for you, Your Highness," said the guard in a winning tone. Ari squirmed in Violet's grip, sure that the guard intended to squish him the moment the princess was out of sight rather than go to the hassle of returning him to the garden.

Thankfully, Violet seemed to suspect the same thing. "Thank you for the offer, but I'm afraid I don't trust you as far as I could throw you," she said cheerfully. "No offense." She looked down at Ari again. "No, I think I'll take responsibility for your safety, little frog."

Was it possible to feel demeaned and deeply comforted at the same time? Apparently it was.

Violet took half a step back the way Ari had come, but then a new voice wafted out from a nearby doorway. She turned, and Ari saw that Basil was striding out of the dining hall, in conversation with his steward.

"Basil!" Violet called, turning back. After a moment's hesitation, she shoved Ari in her pocket. "Sorry little one, but if I don't catch him now, I won't get a chance all afternoon." Her voice became muffled as Ari's entire world was enveloped in fabric. He squirmed around in Violet's pocket, getting into a position where he could breathe. It seemed the most he could hope for in the circumstances.

"Violet, there you are." Basil's voice was also deadened by the layers of Violet's gown, but Ari had no trouble making out his words. "I noticed you didn't make it to lunch. The food is still out."

"Never mind that, I can eat later," Violet told him quickly. "Can I have a word? It will only take a minute."

"Of course," said Basil.

Ari thought he sounded surprised, but most of his attention was on Violet. She seemed uncomfortable again. It was the same unease he'd observed multiple times, and he was amazed he could sense it so tangibly even without being able to see her face. It radiated from her.

Violet began to move, meaning that Ari was being jostled as well as being smothered. Yet he couldn't regret their encounter. He didn't even feel overly guilty about the fact that he was about to eavesdrop on her conversation with her brother. Somehow, when he was an animal, the same rules didn't seem to apply in his mind. It had been that way when he was a swan. If he was about to have the opportunity to discover what was really behind Violet's unease, he'd welcome it. Besides, he honestly wasn't sure he could get out of the pocket if he tried.

Violet walked only a short distance before she stopped, and a door clicked audibly closed. It seemed she and her brother were alone in a room. Or at least, as far as they were aware.

"Is everything all right, Violet?" Basil's voice asked in a muffled tone.

"Better than all right." Even from within her pocket, Ari could tell that Violet's cheerful tone was forced. "I have a solution to our merchant crisis."

"Really?" Basil's hopeful voice told Ari that Wren hadn't overstated how dire was the conflict with the Merchants' Guild. "What solution?"

"It's all about ego, really," Violet said. "As I could tell from the start. Ulrich is the key, and his son Yannick is the way to get through to him."

"Your meetings with Yannick have been productive, then?" Basil asked eagerly.

"They have," Violet confirmed, and Ari could feel her shift her weight from one foot to the other. "Yannick is willing to reason with his father. He's given me his word that he'll convince Ulrich to back down about the Mistran merchants under...certain circumstances."

"What circumstances?" Basil asked, suspicion creeping back into his voice.

"The first of them is that Yannick wishes to come and stay in the castle as a guest for a little while," Violet said. "As soon as possible."

Ari blinked, his bulbous eyes unseeing in the darkness of Violet's pocket. He didn't like the idea of Yannick in the castle. He didn't like it at all. He was honest enough to acknowledge that he'd felt some jealousy when he saw Violet hole herself up with the young merchant a short time before. But it wasn't just his own attraction to Violet that made him frown on the idea. It was also the discomfort he'd observed when Violet interacted with Yannick.

And even disregarding both of those points, it was frankly an odd request. Apparently Basil thought so too.

"Why?" demanded the young king.

"Like I said, it's really all about ego," said Violet, a little too airily. "All the talk of profits is really about influence, and the matter of influence comes back to pride. He wants some recognition, to be made a fuss of."

"That's it?" Basil asked, clearly skeptical.

Violet's skirts lifted as she shrugged, her elbow pressing in to the top of her pocket. "That's the start. We've discussed other measures as well—nothing we wouldn't agree to—but that's his first request."

"As to what we will or won't agree to, I'll reserve judgment," Basil said dryly. "But his request to be invited to the castle we can certainly accommodate. I can draw up an official invitation, pander to his and his father's consequence enough to satisfy even the largest of heads."

Ari could hear Violet's grin in her voice. "I knew you wouldn't get on your high horse about it."

"I have much less interest in my pride than in avoiding a merchants' embargo on the city," Basil said flatly. "You can tell him I'll make it happen."

"I already have, actually," Violet admitted. Again Ari could tell she was grinning. "I was pretty confident of my ability to talk you around."

"Vixen," said Basil without heat. "Thanks Violet, you're doing incredible work with the merchants. I don't know what I'd do without you."

"Of course," Violet replied.

Ari heard the king's firm tread, but it stopped before there was any sound of a door opening.

"I hope you don't misunderstand me when I say that, Violet," Basil said, his voice more serious. "I'm glad of your help, but of course I could manage without you. That's my role, and my responsibility. I don't want you to involve yourself even a moment beyond what you're comfortable with. It's not on your shoulders to solve this crisis."

"It is," said Violet calmly. "And I don't mean that in a critical way. But you delegated the task to me, Basil, and I accepted it. You have to let me follow through. I know you don't want any of us to feel pressured, but the truth is you do need help. You can't do everything by yourself. You told us when Father died that you weren't going to try, that you'd need all the help you can get. But it's as though the curse changed your mind. I know you wish you'd somehow prevented it, but there was nothing you could have done. And it's time to let go of the over-protective determination it created in you to shield us from any inconvenience or responsibility."

Basil's sigh was audible. "You're right," he acknowledged. "And I know I can't do everything by myself. But I meant what I said. I don't want you doing anything you're uncomfortable with."

Violet didn't answer, just fidgeting with a distinct lack of her usual self-possession.

"I'll speak to the steward about accommodating Yannick," said Basil, with a return to his habitual brisk manner. "As soon as is practical."

On this pronouncement Basil left the room in earnest, but Violet stayed where she was. Ari was also motionless, pondering the king's words. Was it just general brotherly protectiveness, overlaid with the guilt Violet had referenced, a lingering effect of the curse that had gripped all twelve of the king's sisters? Or had Basil, like Ari, noticed that Violet seemed uncomfortable whenever the Merchants' Guild came up, or when she spoke of Ulrich and his son Yannick?

Well, whether or not Basil had picked up on it, Ari had. And reclaiming his human form was no longer his only mission, especially if this Yannick was to be staying in the castle itself. Obviously lifting the curse was still his most pressing priority. But in the meantime he would make a point of keeping an eye on this Yannick.

Or to be more precise, two unsettlingly bulging eyes.

# CHAPTER NINE

## Violet

Violet entered the dining hall at a distracted stroll, her mind on her conversation with Basil. She'd set the wheels of her plan in motion. It wouldn't be easy to turn back now. Not that she intended to.

Many of the family had eaten and were getting ready to leave, but as Basil had said, the food was still laid out. It wasn't until Violet sank into a chair and felt something bulge in her pocket that she remembered the poor frog. She hesitated, then felt it squirm into a better position and let herself relax. It had been fine thus far, surely it wouldn't make much difference if she ate first. It wasn't as though it had been trying to fight free of her pocket.

Violet was barely aware of what food she put in her mouth, her thoughts too consumed with the idea of a future with Yannick. She couldn't deny that her heart was heavy. But that was understandable given her recent disappointment regarding Ari. She had no real reason to look on Yannick with anything less than respect. Surely they could build a stable life together, even if not a very exciting one.

Once she'd shoveled down some lunch, Violet made

straight for the gardens on the non-ocean side of the castle. She knew there was a large pond there, and it seemed the best place to deposit the frog. She didn't spend much time in the garden, preferring the ocean views and the sand beneath her feet, but she knew it was a favorite haunt of Wren's. She'd have to ask her sister-in-law if she'd seen many frogs roaming the area.

When Violet reached the pond, however, she encountered a problem. Apparently, the frog had no interest in being dumped back into the water. It came out of her pocket without protest, but when she tried to release it, it clung to her desperately. Any time she managed to get her hand free, it only leaped back onto her skirts, attempting to clamber back into her pocket.

"No, you're free!" she told it, exasperated. "I'm releasing you back to your home. Silly creature, do you want to live in a pocket? This is where you belong!"

Unsurprisingly, the frog was deaf to her words. It continued its determined attempts to remain attached to her person. Violet tried to repel it, but there was only so much she could do while still being gentle enough not to hurt it.

"Come on, frog," she said pleadingly. "This is a very nice pond in a very nice garden. There are lots of bugs for you to eat, trees to shield you from the sun, nice water to paddle in...this garden even has a secret tunnel over there." She gestured vaguely. "It's fit for royalty, come on! How picky a frog are you?"

Still the frog made no move toward the water, just staring unblinkingly up at her.

She rocked back on her heels, frowning down at the amphibian which was now sitting calmly on her lap. Surely this wasn't normal behavior for a frog.

"Do you...do you want to stay with me?" she asked it, bemused.

The frog just blinked its bulbous eyes at her.

"Do I seem that lonely?" she asked it ruefully. "Is it that

obvious that I'm desperate for a friend?" She sighed. "I have no reason to want for companionship," she informed the frog. "I have *twelve* siblings, for goodness' sake!" She looked down at it. It was watching her with an intensity of focus she found strangely comforting. She had its full attention, for whatever that was worth. "And yet, I clearly am wanting for companionship, since I'm pouring out my troubles to a frog."

She couldn't help laughing, both at herself and at the ridiculous amphibian. "Come on, then. I'll put you back in my pocket, just for a bit. Can you even keep frogs as pets? Is that something people do?"

The frog didn't reply, but nor did it resist when she picked it up and slipped it into her pocket.

"You're not as slimy as I expected," she commented, pulling the pocket open so she could peer in at it. "Smooth, but actually quite pleasant to the touch. My congratulations on your cleanliness."

The frog blinked at her, the strange movement of its eyelids equal parts unnerving and entertaining. Chuckling, Violet let the fabric fall closed and started back toward the castle.

The afternoon was mainly taken up with communicating about Yannick's upcoming visit, and assisting with preparations. She caught a few knowing looks from the servants and suspected that some were quicker than Basil had been to understand the reason for the merchant's son being so honored. She told herself not to let it trouble her. What did it matter if gossip went ahead of the event itself? Perhaps she should have been more open with Basil about the true nature of her bargain with Yannick, but she knew for certain he'd object. He'd want to protect her, and in so doing, would ruin the only solution they had for the merchant crisis.

All through her activities, the frog sat happily in her pocket. Occasionally it shifted around, but any time she offered it the chance of exiting her pocket, it showed no inclination to do so.

By the time she made her way to dinner, she was weary, and in no mood to be sociable. She also didn't feel like explaining her sudden acquisition of a pet frog, so she left it where it was. The meal had barely started, however, when her new companion sabotaged that plan.

Zinnia was once again present, with Genny on her lap. Obsidian, however, was still caught up with the Enchanters' Guild. It seemed whatever situation had required his assistance was more demanding than Violet had realized. Zinnia was her usual lively self. She launched into a humorous account of the cool disdain with which Obsidian had apparently set about deflating the ego of some of the more difficult student enchanters. Almost as soon as Zinnia began speaking, the inhabitant of Violet's pocket began to make frantic attempts to get free.

Her gown bulged and shuffled alarmingly, long amphibian legs kicking into her thigh as the frog went berserk trying to find the exit.

"Not now," Violet muttered under her breath. "I'll take you back to the pond, just wait until after dinner."

The frog paid no heed. As Zinnia continued with her tale, it pushed and wriggled with everything it had, eventually succeeding in finding the opening in the fabric. Violet's hand shot down as its squat little head poked out into the fresh air, but she wasn't quick enough. It slipped through her grasp, slithering onto her lap then leaping straight onto the table.

Violet lunged for it, but apparently it wasn't finished. With bizarre determination for a creature which had spent most of the day dormant in her pocket, it hopped its way along the table, heading straight for Zinnia who was still speaking.

It took only moments for the loose amphibian to catch the

attention of Violet's family. Three-year-old Teddy was the first to see it.

"Look, Mama," he said, pointing. "Frog!"

Everyone turned to look, and a chorus of squeals went up. The various reactions directly correlated to the age of the observer. Violet's mother drew back from the table with a genteel little cry of horror, and a few of the older princesses let out gasps or squeaks as they pulled their hands instinctively back from their food and leaned backward in their chairs.

The children, however, were delighted. Their squeals were the loudest, but they showed no sign of withdrawing. Instead, they leaned forward with great excitement, Azure even going so far as to reach one chubby little hand toward the still-hopping frog.

Violet shoved her closest sister out of the way as she slid down the table, trying to catch hold of her little green friend. She'd begun to despair of catching it before someone squished it when it suddenly—and inexplicably—came to a stop. Everyone else paused too, staring warily at the imposter. The frog was sitting still, its front feet splayed and its long back legs bent up under it as it stared from Zinnia to the seats on either side of her. As Violet came to a stop behind her sister's chair, the frog let out a doleful ribbit. The eldest princess had of course stopped speaking in the kerfuffle, and she stared blankly back at the frog.

"Can I help you?" she asked after a prolonged moment of silence, humor tickling her words.

If possible, the frog's eyes bulged even more than usual.

Zinnia was openly grinning now, even as she restrained her daughter from getting too close to the creature. "It seems to like me, doesn't it? Should I keep it as a pet?"

"Too late," said Violet waspishly, taking advantage of the frog's distraction to scoop it back up. It didn't even protest, deflating in her hand into a defeated posture. "I've already adopted it."

A general outcry greeted these words, ranging from demands for information to laughter at what was clearly interpreted as a joke.

"Violet, I trust you're not serious," her mother said when she could make herself heard. "You can't have a *frog* as a pet."

"Why not?" Violet demanded belligerently.

"Because it's…not seemly," her mother said in a helpless way. She looked at her son. "Basil, surely you agree with me."

"I don't see the harm, Mother," said Basil mildly.

"Yes, Mama, Violet needs a new friend," piped up the youngest of Violet's sisters. "Because her sweetheart ran away from her, remember?"

"Thank you, Wisteria," said Violet dryly. "So thoughtful of you."

Wisteria shrugged. "I'm just saying the truth. You can't get me in trouble for that."

"Can't I?" Violet glared threateningly at the eight-year-old, who resumed eating her dinner with complete unconcern.

"Oh, leave her alone, Wisteria," said Basil. Again, his words were light and casual, but Wisteria instantly subsided.

Violet winced. If Basil was coming to her defense, however diplomatically, he clearly thought her in need of shielding. No doubt they all considered her to be languishing under a broken heart.

What nonsense. Mostly.

Cheeks burning, Violet returned the frog to her pocket, bizarrely grateful that she'd been allowed to keep her pet. It was a good thing that Basil had never been in the habit of saying no to his sisters. Since assuming the throne at eighteen, he'd been a much more popular guardian than their father before him, rest the late king's soul.

Violet spent the rest of the meal responding to fascinated questions about how she'd come to adopt a frog, leading her to make her escape as quickly as possible. She couldn't really explain the affection she felt for the creature. On private reflection, the detail that sprang most to mind was the moment by the pond, when the frog had sat on her lap and given her such absolute, unhurried attention. But she didn't say this to her family. It would be too embarrassing to admit that she liked the frog because it had time for her. How pathetic had she become?

When she reached her suite, Violet told the maid who was waiting for her that she would ready herself for bed, not wanting to deal with the girl's reaction when she produced the amphibian from her pocket. As soon as she was alone, she withdrew it, however, placing it on her pillow.

"Where would be comfortable for you to sleep? she asked it thoughtfully. "And you must be hungry." She glanced at the windowsill. "I see a few dead flies there, if that helps." She started to pull her arms free of her dress, and was startled by the frog's sudden motion as it hopped off her bed and across the floor. Before she could stop it, it hopped right into her receiving room, the door of which was standing open.

Violet followed it in, trying to coax it to return. But it had settled itself on the windowsill and refused to budge.

Satisfied that it wasn't trying to escape through the window—there was only a narrow strip of land between the building and a perilous cliff—she returned to her sleeping chamber. Once she was ready for bed, she went back into the receiving room to try again to convince the frog to sleep in her chamber, which had the benefit of a warm fire. She found it munching on a large blowfly that had obviously met its end on the frog's chosen windowsill, not looking as though it was greatly enjoying its meal. She picked it up, but it instantly squirmed free, returning to its position.

After several more attempts, Violet gave up. Perhaps it didn't wish to be her pet. If it preferred to be free, she didn't blame it. She felt guilty for not returning it to the pond, but it was too late now. It was dark, and she was in her nightgown.

Resolving to let the poor animal go emotionally as well as physically, she climbed into her bed, drifting at once into a dreamless slumber.

# CHAPTER TEN

# *Ari*

Ari waited on the windowsill, holding himself tensely until he heard Violet settle into her bed through the open door. Embarrassment rushed over him as he thought of her attempts to get him to sleep next to—perhaps even on—her bed. He'd almost wished that he no longer had his human thoughts. It was all a little too...fraught.

*You're a frog*, he reminded himself. *She thought she was inviting a pet frog into her bed. Not you.*

A thought flicked through his mind. Just how fond of her pet frog was she? Should he perhaps take her up on her offer to sleep right next to her? Was there any chance, however slim, that he could convince her to kiss him? It should break the enchantment.

Ari shook his head, half embarrassed, half amused by his own foolishness. He'd seen people press fond kisses to a favorite puppy, or even a kitten. But a frog? Not likely.

With a ghastly gulp, he swallowed the fly he'd been ingesting. He didn't blame Violet in the least. He felt extraordinarily un-kissable right now. The feeling of the fly sliding down his throat was a horrid sensation. But it did go some way to satisfying the hunger that had gnawed at him throughout the day. Reluctantly, he hunted out a few more around the edges of the room, sucking them down as quickly as possible, so as not to give himself time to think about it.

The curtains were closed, and the room was fairly dark, only dim light making its way in from the fire in Violet's sleeping chamber. But Ari's frog eyes had no difficulty taking everything in. It was quite convenient, really, as he navigated the unfamiliar space. He was just hopping along the edge of a bureau when a glimmer of something caught his eye. He paused, peering down the tiny gap between the bureau and the wall.

Something silver was down there, something that glinted in the muted firelight. The necklace! It must be the necklace Violet had mentioned more than once, the one stuck down the side of a bureau. Ari could see the problem. The bureau sat nearly flush with the wall—even the smallest of human hands would be unable to reach into that gap to retrieve it. And the furniture itself was affixed to the wall.

Ari hopped down onto the floor, creeping forward until he was peering in the side of the bureau. He could see the necklace, coiled up halfway along the space, as thick as a rope to his new size.

One experimental push was enough to convince Ari that the gap was too small to squeeze his amphibian form into. He was just looking at his frog hands, wishing they were more dexterous, when another thought occurred to him.

His tongue! He hadn't tried it out yet, but frogs were supposed to have long and sticky tongues. He poked it out, feeling foolish. The results were unimpressive. Ari closed his eyes, forcing his mind to turn to the flies he'd just consumed. He tried to silence his thoughts, instead encouraging his new instincts. He imagined a buzzing fly, meandering over the pond, unsuspecting of danger.

*Flick!*

His tongue shot out seemingly of its own accord, sticking to the bureau so securely he had to peel it back with some force.

Excellent. Repositioning himself, Ari tried the same maneuver, this time taking aim into the gap. It took a few tries, but he managed to get his tongue to latch on to the silver coil. When he retracted it, the necklace came too, a little dusty, but undamaged.

Trying to ignore the unpleasantness of the metal taste in his mouth, Ari hopped across the floor, heading for the open door into Violet's sleeping chamber. He hesitated in the doorway, his superior eyes searching the gloom until they landed on Violet's form. She was still and peaceful, clearly in a deep slumber.

Moving quietly, Ari leaped onto a footstool, then up again onto the dresser that sat by the window. Carefully, he deposited the necklace on the wooden surface, then turned toward the bed. As stealthily as his jerky movements would allow, he crept from one item of furniture to another, until he was close enough to properly observe Violet.

She had a very appealing face, the laugh lines visible even in the relaxation of sleep. And in spite of its tousled state, her hair framed her head perfectly, falling in thick brown waves. She was very beautiful.

*And very unaware of being observed,* he reminded himself. Guiltily, he hopped away, returning to his post in the receiving room. His body was on high alert, but his mind was weary. He would have to be disciplined with his sleep rhythm if he wanted to spend the day with Violet rather than sleeping under a log somewhere.

Ari was woefully conscious of being no closer to his goal of lifting the enchantment than he had been that morning. He'd felt so hopeful when he heard Zinnia speaking, sure that Obsidian would be with her and the enchanter would be able to help him. It had been bitterly disappointing to realize that the princess's husband wasn't present. But after all, what was one more day?

In spite of his absurd and alarming predicament, Ari couldn't help feeling a little pleased. It seemed that even in frog form, he managed to catch not only the attention but the favor of Violet.

That was something, after all.

---

Ari woke to the sound of movement in the next room. It took him a moment to get his bearings. The basin in which he'd slept wasn't the most comfortable of beds, and he stretched out each of his legs one at a time. He'd just hopped out onto a table when he heard a cry of surprise. Tentatively, he moved forward, wondering if it would be an invasion of privacy for him to go into the sleeping chamber.

Before he'd decided, the door to the corridor swung open, and a maid walked confidently across the receiving room. Ari drew back out of sight as the girl entered the princess's sleeping chamber, pulling up in surprise in the doorway.

"You're already up and dressed, Your Highness!"

"Yes," came Violet's voice, sounding distracted. "Look at this! I didn't even notice it last night."

"The necklace, Your Highness?" The servant sounded confused.

Ari moved forward in time to see Violet's beaming face as she held the item out for the other girl to see.

"It was stuck down the bureau. Basil must have found a

way to get it out without shifting the furniture. And to think I've been secretly annoyed with him for not getting to it." Her eyes shifted past the maid, her face brightening as her gaze fell on Ari's miniature form. "You're still here!"

The maid turned in confusion, giving a little shriek when she saw who the princess was speaking to.

"Stars above, how did a frog get in here? I'll deal with it, Your Highness, not to worry."

"No, no, leave it be," said Violet, laughing. "The frog is a friend of mine."

Ignoring the maid's startled protests, Violet scooped Ari up, placing him on her shoulder.

"This gown doesn't have pockets," she informed him sagely, as she strode out into the corridor. "But perhaps it's for the best. Surely you don't want to be smothered all day."

Ari clung on to the fabric of Violet's sleeve with grim determination, swaying alarmingly as she walked. She was right that it was nice to be able to breathe freely. But she clearly had no idea how precarious his position was.

His appearance created a sensation at breakfast, all the younger ones overjoyed to see Violet's pet frog return. Violet actually had to move seats halfway through the meal, as she'd made the tactical mistake of sitting too close to her youngest niece. Azure was determined to get hold of Ari, and he could only be grateful Violet was vigilant in protecting him.

"I love her to bits, but she'd squish you with one squeeze if given the chance," Violet informed him, a pronouncement with which Ari silently agreed.

After the first ten minutes, everyone seemed to accept Ari's presence, returning their focus to their food. Ari hovered on Violet's shoulder, listening with interest to the various conversations. It was a fascinating experience to be the proverbial fly on the wall. He could see that Wren was troubled, most likely about his disappearance. He contemplated hopping over to her to try to communicate. But how would he do that? He couldn't speak, he couldn't write. And Azure was still perched on Wren's lap, as effective as a bodyguard.

The rest of the family chatted about various topics with their usual chaotic volume, often only hearing half of what was being said to them. Violet asked for someone to pass the salt five separate times—trying three different people—before Ari lost patience and leaped down from her shoulder.

Hopping across the table, he once again employed his overlong, sticky tongue. It shot out with a speed that even he found abrupt, curling around the salt cellar and bringing it zipping back to him. He turned to Violet, depositing it in front of her.

This simple act caused a sensation. All his admirers were delighted with his performance, while those who disapproved of him protested that Violet should keep her unclean pet away from the food at the very least.

Violet, on the other hand, stared at him in astonishment. Likely no one else had even heard her requests for the salt, so to them Ari's actions were random and entertaining. But Violet must be very aware that he'd only leaped into motion after she'd repeatedly and unsuccessfully tried to get her hands on the salt cellar.

Ari stared back at Violet, not entirely sure what he was hoping for, but not trying to look like a normal frog, either. He tried nodding his head, as if in confirmation of whatever thoughts she was having about his abnormal behavior. But the movement didn't feel right at all. He doubted it looked anything like a human nod.

After a moment, Violet just shook her head, putting him back on her shoulder before seizing the salt.

"Thanks, I guess?" she said. Ari wasn't sure whether she'd

decided it was a coincidence, or whether she was reserving judgment.

In any event, he spent the rest of the day traveling around the castle with Violet, either on her shoulder or sitting on her outstretched hand. From what he overheard, Yannick was due to arrive at the castle the following day, but for the moment Violet's time was her own. She no longer tried to hide him, and gossip quickly spread about the princess's bizarre new pet. He sat openly at the table at meals, and by dinner time he was such a fixture that she even offered him food off her plate.

Ari accepted gratefully, which seemed to surprise Violet. He honestly had no idea whether his body would be able to digest the human fare, but he decided he'd rather try it and face the consequences than choke down any more flies. The dowager queen's horror at this development was made comical by the teasing directed at her by all her children. Everyone else had gotten over their astonishment, apparently deciding to be amused by their sister's new quirk.

That evening was spent much the same as the one before, Ari rejecting all attempts to get him to share Violet's sleeping quarters, opting instead to settle down in the receiving room. When breakfast the following morning was once again conspicuously missing both Zinnia and Obsidian, Ari decided it was time to formulate a new plan. He'd obviously overestimated how often the married couple dined at the castle with the family. Waiting for Obsidian to appear and magically recognize him was no longer a sensible course.

Ari was just debating—while riding around on Violet's shoulder—whether to try to find out where Obsidian lived or to come up with an entirely different approach, when a distraction occurred.

Several of the younger princesses had gone down the cliff path to the beach, as was apparently a common pastime. One of them, whose name Ari couldn't remember, came racing into the castle, sand flying from her skirts and eyes wide.

"Goodness, Dahlia, what's going on?" Violet asked her, as the younger girl skidded to a halt.

"They're back," gasped Dahlia. "Both of them."

"Who's back?" Violet asked blankly.

"The dragons!"

Violet stiffened at her sister's reply, and Ari could feel the excitement racing through her. "Dannsair and Rekavidur?"

Dahlia nodded breathlessly.

"We need to send a message to Zinnia," said Violet. "She won't want to miss this." She flagged down a passing servant, repeating the news and instructing him to notify the eldest princess in her home. She didn't even wait for the servant to acknowledge her before seizing Dahlia's hand and racing toward the door, Ari clinging precariously to her shoulder.

"What's brought them back?" she wondered aloud. "You're sure it's them, and not some other dragons?"

"Of course I'm sure," said Dahlia scornfully. "Do you think I could fail to recognize Reka and Dannsair? They're our *friends*."

Violet didn't sound as confident. "I'm not sure humans can ever truly be friends with dragons. But I know what you mean. They're much more approachable than other dragons. I think they're genuinely fond of Zinnia, at least."

"And all of us," said Dahlia, sounding offended.

Violet didn't comment, although Ari could sense her skepticism.

"I wonder where they've been," she mused, as they left the castle and hurried toward the cliff and the downward path. "They haven't come to Entolia for years. I don't think I've seen them since our curse was lifted." She shook her head, her hair whipping Ari in the face. "I doubt they'll tell us what they've been up to. They might not be as aloof as most dragons, but they're still dragons."

As they crested the cliff and started their descent, Ari's already protuberant eyes widened. He'd seen dragons before, plenty of times. His home city of Myst wasn't far from the dragon colony, and they often flew overhead. But he'd rarely seen them up this close, or this relaxed.

Because the two dragons down on the shore looked as relaxed as house cats in a patch of sunlight. They were small as dragons went, meaning they were relatively young—probably less than a century. They were still several times taller than a human, though. The other detail that marked their relative youth was the brightness of their scales, which Ari knew would steadily darken throughout their lifespan. One was yellow, with scales tinged with purple, and the other was all purple. They matched well, he reflected. And a good thing, too, if they were the ones he'd heard Wren mention, the ones who had a special sort of semi-friendship with the Entolian princesses. He knew those dragons to be a pair, mated for their whole immortal lives.

The yellow one was stretched out across the surface of the water, its head resting on one protruding rock, and its belly on another. Bearded ridges ran along its temples, and Ari's eyes followed the triangular spikes which ran from the back of its neck all the way down its tail. Or at least, down as much of its tail as he could see, given the end of it dangled into the water.

The purple one was currently sitting back on its haunches on a large flat rock partially out to sea. Its head was bent low, apparently in conversation with those of Violet's sisters who were ranged along the sandy shore, staring eagerly up at the dragon. When Violet and Dahlia arrived on the beach, the dragon transferred its attention to them.

"Greetings, Princess Violet," the dragon said. By the sound of its voice, this one was the female.

"Greetings, Dannsair," said Violet, dipping her head respectfully. Her gaze traveled out to the other dragon. "Greetings, Rekavidur."

He lifted his head, nodding serenely in acknowledgment. "Greetings, Princess Violet."

One of the other princesses piped up, probably continuing the conversation they'd interrupted, and Ari settled in to observe the dragons. To his discomfort, he realized that the yellow one out to sea was observing him back.

"Is that a frog on your shoulder, Princess Violet?" the dragon, Rekavidur, asked.

"Yes," said Violet, the word sounding defensive to Ari. Acting on some instinct of caution, he shuffled closer to her neck. "It's my new...pet."

The dragon raised his head fully, narrowing his orb-like eyes as he stared at Ari. "That is an odd pet. I find it...offensive."

Ari could feel Violet's surprise, and for a moment, no one spoke. It was a testament to the friendship the princesses claimed with the dragons that no one immediately abased themselves in apology, or even fled fearfully. That was how most humans would react to being told they'd offended a dragon.

"Do you agree, Dannsair?" Rekavidur appealed to the other dragon.

She lowered her head, sniffing in Violet and Ari's general direction. "Yes, I have the same reaction," she assured her pair.

"Well," said Violet stiffly. "I'm sure it wasn't my intention to offend anyone. Although I don't know why you would care about my choice of pet."

Rekavidur's scales rippled in the dragon equivalent of a shrug, no particular heat in his voice. "You will suit yourself, I understand. It does not after all affect us. But I consider your choice of pet ill-advised."

"Thank you for your opinion," said Violet, not managing to hide how affronted she was. She dropped into a full curtsy this time, causing Ari to wobble dangerously on his perch. Then, with a painfully formal leave-taking, she turned back toward the cliff path.

She was only halfway up it when Zinnia came tumbling down, her eyes alight with excitement.

"Reka, Dannsair!" she cried. "Where have you been? You missed my wedding!"

Ari was curious about how the dragons would receive this exuberance, but he didn't dare swivel to watch. He didn't wish to attract any more attention from the fearsome beasts—the attention he'd already garnered was alarming enough. If he'd been worried about a one-year-old squishing him by accident, the threat of a dragon's displeasure was nothing short of catastrophic.

Violet said nothing as they reached the top of the path and headed toward the castle. After all, who would she speak to? She didn't know her frog could understand her. They were just re-entering the castle when a servant hurried up to them, bowing to Violet.

"Your Highness, I was sent in search of you. I'm to notify you that Yannick has arrived."

"Oh, of course," said Violet, snapping out of her disgruntled reverie. "I'll receive him in the yellow room."

"Yes, Your Highness," said the servant. His eyes flicked to Ari then rapidly away before he bowed again. "At once."

Violet waited until he was out of sight, but then she turned to Ari with a sigh. "He's right in his unspoken disapproval," she informed him reluctantly. "I probably shouldn't go to meet Yannick with you perched on my shoulder. First the dragons, then the merchants. It seems no one approves of our connection, my friend."

Robbed of any other communication, Ari let out a sad ribbit.

Violet's lips twitched as she carefully lifted him from her shoulder, sliding him back into the oblivion of her pocket. At least today's gown had a pocket.

Their progress through the castle became considerably harder to track after that point, but it wasn't many minutes later that Violet sank into a seat, causing Ari to shuffle frantically in her pocket to avoid being squashed. He wasn't nearly as hardy—and she wasn't nearly as cautious of him—as she seemed to think.

It seemed that Yannick was shown into the room mere moments later, because Violet rose again.

"Welcome," she said, her tone polite but formal. "I trust your accommodations are to your liking?"

"Very much so, Your Highness," came Yannick's muffled voice. It was the first time Ari had heard him speak, and he didn't warm to the young merchant. Perhaps he was prejudiced, but his first impression of the other man was one of smugness. "You've been very gracious in your accommodations."

The conversation was mercifully short, neither giving the impression that they had any desire to linger in the other's company. Apparently this meeting was a matter of formality. Even the little Yannick said reinforced Ari's original impression, however. He just couldn't shake the feeling that the young merchant was well-satisfied with his situation. Ari didn't trust him at all.

When the pair parted ways, Ari hesitated for only a moment before making his decision. He knew where to find Violet, but he might not have much opportunity to observe

Yannick. He had no idea how the guest was to be entertained during his visit. It was possible their paths wouldn't cross much. This might be his best chance to make good on his private determination to keep an eye on the other man.

With difficulty, he struggled from Violet's pocket, pausing when his head was poking out through the fabric.

"You all right, little pal?" Violet asked in an undertone, clearly not wanting to draw Yannick's attention. Ari could still see Yannick's back, but he'd almost disappeared around a corner.

Without pausing to respond to Violet—not that he could— Ari sprung from her pocket, using his back legs to propel himself off her thigh. She let out a muted cry and grabbed at him, but he was too fast. He hopped down the corridor with purpose, rounding the corner and bringing Yannick back into sight. If Violet pursued him now, she'd have to accept the merchant witnessing her retrieval of her controversial pet. Ari wasn't surprised when she didn't do so.

He followed Yannick as clandestinely as speed would allow, noting that the other man was definitely going somewhere. He wasn't just wandering. Was he meeting someone? Or just returning to whatever luxurious suite he'd been assigned?

Ari had trailed Yannick down several corridors, all the while growing more convinced that Yannick was in a hurry to meet someone, when he saw something that distracted him completely.

Yannick was striding past a connecting corridor when he suddenly faltered, his head darting to the side before he straightened and resumed his walk. Following his gaze, Ari could understand why he'd been startled. The figure hovering in the other corridor was so still Ari had missed him at first, and it was unnerving to realize someone was watching him pass unseen. He was just reflecting that it looked suspiciously like lurking when he realized the man's identity and faltered to a stop.

Lex!

It hadn't been obvious at first—after all, he was used to looking the other man in the eye rather than staring up at him in giant form from the floor. But now he was paying attention, there was no mistaking the loyal Mistran servant. Ari hesitated, surprise and confusion temporarily driving Yannick's destination from his mind.

What was Lex still doing here? When the servant had asked to return to Myst rather than travel on to Bansford with Ari, he'd assumed the older man meant to depart the next morning. Ari was aware that Lord Golding had left for Myst the day after Ari's disappearance, to take word of his defection to his parents. So why would Lex be lingering in the Entolians' castle days after the guest he was attending had departed? Was he just staying on until he received confirmation of what had happened to Ari? Ari knew from what he'd overheard that the almost universally held opinion was that he'd taken off to Bansford on his own as a lark. But perhaps Lex wasn't convinced.

Unthinkingly, Ari hopped toward his servant, out of long-held habit. Lex had been a source of assistance and sympathy many times. Surely he could help Ari. He propelled himself upward, his jerky movements still awkward, although they were much more controlled than they had been at first.

But when he landed on Lex's arm, the other man showed no inclination to help. He didn't even respond with the sympathy that Violet had shown on first seeing Ari in his amphibian form.

"Urgh, get off!" said the Mistran sharply. He swatted at Ari, dislodging him and sending him to the floor with a splat. "Get away, I say." The servant's voice dropped to a mutter. "What kind of royals let frogs roam through their castle? Degenerates."

Still muttering, he strode away, leaving Ari dazed and disappointed. When his head stopped spinning, he realized that the worst of it was that Lex's distraction had cost him his chance to follow Yannick. The younger man was nowhere to be seen, and a quick search confirmed that Ari had lost his trail. If the merchant's son had been going to meet someone, Ari would never know their identity now.

Disheartened, Ari hopped his way back through the castle, his progress slow due to the need to avoid being seen by any zealous guard or servant, most of whom would as soon squish him as look at him.

Not knowing where else to go, he made his way to the dining hall, concealing himself in a plant pot until the dinner hour. The wait felt interminable, but eventually the royal family started to trickle into the room. Ari's eyes latched on to Violet the moment she appeared, noting that she looked downcast.

Was it his departure, the real him? Or perhaps the arrival of Yannick, whom he was still convinced made her uncomfortable? Or maybe even the loss of her pet frog?

Absurd as it all was, the latter guess seemed the most likely, judging by her response when Ari hopped out of hiding.

"You came back!" Violet cried, scooping him up with delight. She turned to see her family staring at her like she'd lost her mind, but it didn't seem to bother her. She beamed at them all, taking her seat and depositing Ari next to her plate. "The frog is back, everybody, no need to panic."

"Oh good, we'll stop lying awake in concern," muttered one of the other princesses sarcastically.

Violet just grinned at her, offering Ari bits of food as the meal commenced, devolving rapidly into the usual pandemonium. Once again Ari witnessed Violet's silent frustration at the impossibility of getting anyone's attention amid the clamor. Her excitement over his frog self's reappearance quickly faded, replaced with the discomfort that seemed to so often follow her these days.

Ari frowned internally as he gobbled up a choice morsel of fish, revising his first impression about which of the possible reasons had her depressed. Perhaps it was all three. His thoughts flew to the merchant's son who seemed to create such discomfort in Violet. She was a smart girl—if Yannick made her uneasy, there was a reason. Ari once again scolded himself for losing the opportunity to see what Yannick was up to, resolving to make more of an effort the next chance he got.

Conversation was still going at full volume when the sweets were served, but Violet seemed weary of it. She'd just placed some kind of cream-filled pastry on her plate and was reaching for her fork when the sister sitting next to her—no older than ten, by the look of her—gestured wildly in illustration of her point and sent Violet's fork clattering to the floor in the process.

The girl talked on, apparently not even aware that she'd knocked her sister's silverware. With a long-suffering sigh, Violet leaned down to retrieve it.

But Ari was quicker. His heart moved out of all proportion to this insignificant setback, he leaped from the table, landing beside the fork with a squelch. Using his tongue, he secured the fork, then leaped back up onto Violet's lap.

Taken aback, she took the fork from him. Her eyes softened a little as she looked his diminutive form over.

"Thanks, frog friend," she said quietly. In spite of reclaiming her utensil, she didn't show much interest in her pastry. After only a couple of bites, she excused herself from the table, placing Ari on her shoulder as she made her way toward her suite.

Ari hovered in the receiving room as usual while Violet prepared herself for bed. But once she was settled, he found himself creeping back into her room, against his better judgment. He knew it wasn't good form to be in her sleeping chamber when she didn't know there was a human mind inside the frog's body, but his intention was very much chivalrous rather than the reverse.

"Hey little frog friend," Violet said softly. Her voice reflected the weariness Ari had seen on her face when she rose from the table. "At least there's someone who hears and sees me."

She chuckled as she said it, as if even in front of a frog she felt the need to pretend the words were lighthearted.

But Ari's heart ached a little because, frog or not, he could tell that at their core, they were anything but.

# CHAPTER ELEVEN

## *Violet*

Violet woke abruptly, to the sound of a scream coming from her receiving room. She could see the weak morning sunlight streaming through the open curtains, but it still took her a moment to get her bearings. Why did her instincts tell her to race to the rescue without a moment's delay?

"Get away, you nasty frog!"

Violet shot upright at the sound of the voice, her mind catching up fully. Her frog! The maid would squish it if she didn't intervene.

"Stop!" she cried, throwing herself toward the door into her receiving room. "Stop, the frog is with me."

"The frog is...what, Your Highness?" It was Naomi who was in the other room, and she sounded understandably confused.

Violet opened her mouth to explain even as her eyes searched the space frantically for the frog. There he was, retreating hastily across an armchair and clearly unharmed. Relieved, she let her gaze fly back to Naomi, and her explanation died on her lips. She'd expected to see the maid stoking the fire, or pulling back the curtains. But Naomi was behind Violet's desk, looking almost like the frog had caught her in the act of, well, snooping.

For a moment, Violet considered saying something, then decided against it. Most likely Naomi had retreated back there to get away from the frog. She didn't want to be the type of harsh mistress who was always accusing the servants of wrongdoing without any evidence.

"It's all right, Naomi," she said soothingly. "The frog is a sort of pet of mine. Just leave him be, he's quite tame."

As she moved back into her bedroom, she caught sight of two large shapes drifting over the ocean through the open window. Hmph. Rekavidur and Dannsair were back, were they? Hopefully they'd keep their opinions to themselves this time.

Once Naomi had helped her prepare herself for the day, Violet wandered back into her receiving room, looking for her frog. It was sitting on a small side table, waiting patiently for her. With a smile, she picked it up, placing it on her shoulder as she walked out into the corridor.

She'd slept later than intended, and she knew she would be expected at breakfast by now. Yannick had been invited to eat luncheon with the family, and she wanted the chance to lecture the younger girls on not letting their tongues run away with them when someone outside the family was present. Although there probably wasn't much point, she reflected glumly. He would be family soon enough, at which point there would be no real reason to keep personal matters from him.

Somehow the thought of bringing Yannick into the intimate family circle was even more depressing than the thought of marrying him. Violet couldn't help thinking wistfully of how comfortably Ari had fit right in. Everyone had liked him, and he'd seemed pleased to be among them. Of course he was Wren's brother, so that gave him an advantage. But Wren had been the same, and Obsidian. The family had been very fortunate with their members by marriage so far. Was she about to break that streak by forming a marriage with no foundation in affection?

She was so lost in her thoughts, she was paying little attention to where she was going. Rounding a corner abruptly, she almost walked right into someone.

"Yannick," she said blankly, rattled to be confronted with the very person she'd been thinking about. "Good morning."

"Good morning, Princess." Yannick bowed respectfully. "I beg your pardon; I didn't see you there."

"No, I'm the one who should apologize," said Violet, waving her hand vaguely. "Do you need something? Was breakfast provided to you?"

"It was," said Yannick comfortably. "I'm not in search of assistance. Just going for a stroll to enjoy the morning air."

"Oh," said Violet, glad not to feel obliged to invite him to join her for the meal. "That's...good."

Fully aware that she wasn't presenting at her most intelligent, she dipped her head in farewell. "I'll see you at noon as planned."

Yannick nodded, giving no sign of wanting her to linger. Violet saw the moment his eyes landed on the frog on her shoulder, causing his mouth to fall slightly open. Violet didn't know whether to grimace or laugh. He would think she'd lost her mind, but it shouldn't make a difference. Not when he was marrying her purely for her crown. She had no intention of giving up her pet for him.

To her dismay, however, her frog was apparently not as committed to this philosophy as she was. As soon as she started walking away from Yannick, the frog swiveled in position, its protruding eyes fixed on the young merchant. Violet looked as well, to see that Yannick was already striding down the corridor. The next thing she knew, the frog had leaped off her shoulder, hitting the stone floor with a quiet splat. Before she could catch it, it hopped toward Yannick, moving with unmistakable purpose.

Violet hesitated, staring after the frog in confusion. The creature had run—or rather hopped—away from her the day before as well. She hadn't connected it with Yannick's arrival at the time, but it seemed a strange coincidence that twice in a row now, the frog had been eager to leave her immediately after she'd met with the young merchant.

Was it...was it following Yannick?

That couldn't be the case. It made no sense. It was the second day in a row, but after all, the frog hadn't been around for long. Maybe it was simply reaching the end of its patience with being domesticated. A bit sad if so, but perfectly under-standable. It was a frog, after all.

Telling herself that the frog would come back if it wanted to —and *trying* to tell herself that she didn't care much either way —Violet continued on to breakfast. She arrived to find half the family already gone. Wren and Basil were both present, prob-ably having been delayed from commencing the meal due to some state matter.

Or perhaps some family matter, Violet reflected, noting that neither of the children were with them.

"Good morning," she greeted her sister-in-law as she helped herself to some boiled eggs.

"What? Oh, good morning, Violet." Wren's distraction made Violet pause, eyeing the other woman with concern.

"Is everything all right?"

"Yes, I'm sure it is," said Wren. "I'm just worried about being late. We're expected for the ceremonial opening of that new market."

"I forgot that was this morning," Violet commented, buttering her toast. "Don't let me keep you."

"You're not," Wren assured her, sinking into the closest chair. "It's the children. We're all supposed to take part in the grand opening—it's their first public appearance in months. They had their breakfast an hour ago, and then some of the nursemaids took them for a walk. They're supposed to be here by now, and I'm not sure which direction they went in order to chase them down."

"How frustrating," said Violet sympathetically, although most of her attention was on her food. She'd just polished off a boiled egg and moved on to a second one when the door opened and Wren relaxed beside her.

"Ah, here they are."

Violet looked up to see one of the children's familiar nursemaids hurrying into the room, Azure clutched in her arms. But no second child appeared behind them, and it only took a glance back at the nursemaid's face to see that something was wrong.

"Where's Teddy?" Wren asked, rising at once and moving forward to meet the nursemaid.

"I...I don't know, Your Majesty," said the girl, looking like it took all her willpower not to burst into tears. "He...he got away from us."

"Got away from you?" Basil entered the conversation, leaving his steward on the other side of the room and crossing the space in a few swift strides. "What does that mean?"

"We were in the garden," the nursemaid said miserably. "And he was playing right there, I swear. But then I turned around, and he was gone. We called and called, and the guards are still searching everywhere, but there's no sign of him."

"Basil, the pond." Wren's face was ashen as she turned horrified eyes to her husband.

"No, Your Majesty, he didn't fall in the water," said the nursemaid vehemently. "I'm sure of it. I was between the pond and the children all the time, and the other girl has stayed there to guard the water's edge just in case. It beats me what happened. He just...disappeared. But he can't have gone far. He's such a little fellow...he must be close."

"Send another squadron of guards," said Basil curtly, addressing one of his personal guards who was standing to attention by the door. Wren hastened to take Azure from the nursemaid as Basil turned to his steward. "We'll have to postpone the market opening. We're not going anywhere until Prince Teddy has been found."

"Of course, Your Majesty," said the steward, looking as worried as Violet felt. "I'll discover which servants were near the area, in case your guards wish to question them."

"Good thought," said Basil, nodding as he strode toward the door.

"Where are you going, Basil?" the dowager queen asked in a strained voice.

"To search the gardens," said Basil. He disappeared through the door on the words, Wren right behind him. Their departure was like a signal for the rest of the family currently in the room, all of whom surged out of their seats and started to follow.

"Hold on!" Lilac called, grabbing two of her youngest sisters by the arms. "Not all of us. You'll just confuse the scene."

"But if there are more of us looking, there's more chance of finding him!" said twelve-year-old Cassia appealingly.

Lilac's expression was grim. "That's true if he's just wandered off. But if he was taken by someone, the guards' job will be harder with so many of us underfoot."

"Do you really think he was taken by someone?" asked nine-year-old Holly in a faint voice.

"I don't know," said Lilac simply. "But we should act like he was, just in case. Here, I'll stay with you."

She looked up and met Violet's eye, the two sisters

exchanging a nod. They were the only adults among the princesses—with the exception of the absent Zinnia—and she was grateful to Lilac for thinking of the practical details. For her part, she fully intended to join the search.

By the time she reached the gardens, the whole place was alive with movement. Violet's heart sank as she took in the bustle of servants and guards combing the area. If Teddy had just wandered off, there was no way he would still be undiscovered by now. The gardens weren't that large. At least one of the original nursemaids was still zealously guarding the pond, as the other one had said. It seemed unlikely that the three-year-old prince had drowned, and that was a huge relief.

Wren and Basil were together, deep in conversation with Basil's head guard, Wren still clutching Azure to her like she'd never let her daughter go. Violet's heart wrenched at the sight of her brother's colorless face. He must have reached the same conclusion as she had about the impossibility of Teddy remaining lost with all these searchers. He wasn't lost. He'd been stolen.

*Who would do something like that?* Violet raged silently. But it was a foolish question. She'd grown up a princess. She knew that royal children were a target for all kinds of mischief. And Teddy was the king's direct heir. He was in much more danger than Violet had ever been as the fourth-born. That was why he and his sister were usually so well guarded. How had someone managed to gain access to them in such a protected place? And where could they have taken him so quickly? The garden led back into the castle, which teemed with guards and servants. There was one outer door, but she knew it was permanently locked, and had been for many years.

Violet's eyes passed across the garden, taking in the pond where she'd tried without success to deposit her frog the first day she found it. She rarely spent time in the garden now, but she used to play there when she was a child. She and Zinnia had been very taken with the idea of the secret tunnel, in spite of it being boarded up and unusable for its original purpose.

The secret tunnel! Violet straightened, hurrying over to Basil. It was a long shot, given how few people even knew about it, but it was definitely worth checking. It was even possible that Teddy had stumbled into it by accident—it was the one place the searchers might not have found him.

"Basil, has anyone checked the tunnel?" she demanded, cutting across whatever the king was saying to his guard.

"What tunnel?" Basil demanded, his wife looking equally confused.

"You know, the one our great-uncle used to use to..." Violet glanced at Azure and cleared her throat. "The one we played in as children."

"I don't remember playing in any tunnel," said Basil blankly.

Violet frowned. "Did you never join us? I suppose you were too busy being the heir. But Zinnia and I did, many times. It started in this garden and led out under the wall."

"What?" Basil's hand clenched into a fist. "You're saying there's a tunnel leading out of the castle grounds that I'm *not* aware of?"

"No, no, it's fully boarded up," said Violet quickly. "It originally led out of castle grounds, but it hasn't been functional for years. Since before we were born."

"But if someone knew about it, could they just remove the boards?" Wren asked anxiously.

Violet shook her head. "Boarded up is the wrong expression. It's properly sealed with stone and everything. Trust me, Zinnia and I tried to get through. It's a dead end. And no one knows about it, anyway. It's a shameful royal secret given its original purpose. But I wondered if Teddy might have found the entrance and wandered in."

"It's worth checking," said Basil tightly, his tone suggesting he wasn't going to allow himself to hope. He gestured for Violet to lead, and she hurried across the garden, trying to remember the way after so many years.

"It comes off this rocky area," she said over her shoulder. She ducked down and crawled inside the entrance to a weeping willow, Basil following on his hands and knees right behind her. "Zinnia and I thought it was brilliant, because we didn't leave obvious tracks for our minders to follow. Once we pulled these branches back down, no one would guess we were there."

As she spoke, she lifted the branches on the far side of the willow. The tree had looked like it was growing right up against an outcropping of stone, but when she pulled the branches away, a small opening was revealed.

Basil practically shoved Violet aside to stick his head into the opening. "Teddy?" he called, his voice somewhere between fear and hope. "Teddy, are you in there?"

Violet frowned, meeting Basil's eye as he swung his head around to face her.

"Did you hear something?" he asked, and she nodded.

"I think so. But it's hard to tell. It didn't sound like a voice so much as shuffling."

"I'm going in," said Basil curtly.

He shouted a command to the guards outside the willow, and he'd barely disappeared into the fissure when someone produced a lantern. Violet snatched it up, following her brother into the tunnel while Wren waited just outside with Azure.

Memories flooded back as Violet crawled forward, of the hours she and Zinnia had hidden in here. The tunnel went for a considerable distance before it was blocked up. She wanted to hope Teddy was in here, but she couldn't escape the obvious question—if he was, why wouldn't he have answered his father's call?

By the time they drew near to the end of the tunnel, Violet was so choked with her fears that she hardly knew what to feel when Basil suddenly cried out ahead of her. Leaning around him, she tried to peer past his shoulder. She let out a strangled gasp at the sight of Teddy, his big brown eyes wide with fear and relief, and his mouth silenced by a strong hand.

"Let him go!" Basil roared, and somewhat to Violet's surprise, the man holding Teddy released him at once.

He was vaguely familiar, but she couldn't immediately place him. Basil reached out as best he could in the enclosed space, grabbing his son and negotiating the boy behind him. Violet seized her nephew at once, murmuring comforting words to him as she shuffled awkwardly backwards, beginning the slow process of getting out of the tunnel and leaving Basil to deal with the unknown man.

When the pair emerged back into the garden, Wren fell on her son with a cry, and Violet hastened to take Azure. For a moment there was chaos as the word rapidly spread that the prince had been found, and Violet had to struggle to make herself heard.

"He wasn't lost," she said, directing her words to both Wren and the head guard hovering nearby. "There was a man with him."

The guard's eyes lit with alarm at the realization that his sovereign was still in the tunnel with a hostile stranger, but a moment later, Basil's feet appeared from the opening, the rest of him following swiftly. Violet expected the other man to be skulking back in the tunnel, but he emerged the next moment, ashen-faced and shaking. He must have thought he could avoid detection in the admittedly excellent hiding place, and had retained enough sense to realize that once he was found, he was backed into a corner.

"Lex?" Wren's cry was half shock, half betrayal. "*You* took Teddy? You kidnapped my son?"

*Lex.* Violet drew in a sharp breath. That was why the man looked familiar. He was the servant who'd come with Ari. The one the Mistran prince had described as one of his family's oldest and most faithful servants.

No wonder Wren felt betrayed.

"I would never hurt him, Your Highness," the older man pleaded brokenly, reverting to the title Wren had carried before she married Basil. "It was never the plan to hurt him. It was all that merchant's son's idea, and I made sure I was the one to take responsibility for the young prince, so I could make sure no harm came to him. Truly, I would never hurt him!"

"Merchant's son?" Violet repeated, the color draining from her face. "Do you mean...do you mean Yannick?"

The old servant said nothing, having apparently regained control of his tongue. But his wary expression seemed to Violet all the answer she needed. She met Basil's eyes, horrified apology in her own. She'd orchestrated Yannick being welcomed into the castle, treated like an honored guest!

"Do you know where he is now?" Basil asked her.

Violet shook her head, her stomach churning. "Not exactly. But I passed him on the way to breakfast. He was on the second floor, heading east in the general direction of the library."

With a curt order, Basil sent guards in search of Yannick, then turned back to Lex.

"If the plan wasn't to harm my son, then what was it?" the king growled, his lithe form bristling with menace. "What were you going to do to him?"

Lex's face hardened now that he was facing Basil instead of

Wren. "The child was safe with me. I would never harm a Mistran royal."

"I don't have the patience for this," Basil snapped. He waved an arm. "Take him to the dungeons." The guards dragged Lex away, impervious to his struggles.

"You've no one to blame but yourself!" the Mistran servant cried, the words clearly directed at Basil. "It's your lax security that allows spies to roam your castle at will."

Basil gave no response. As soon as the accused man was out of sight, he drooped, wrapping his arms around his wife and son. Azure tried to wriggle free, but Violet kept a firm hold on her. The last thing anyone needed right now was for the irrepressible toddler to wander off.

The general mood of the crowd was shocked relief, but Violet's unease was still raging. And it wasn't just because of her guilt over failing so terribly to read Yannick's true intentions.

"Basil, Wren," she said, trying a few times before she caught their attention. "What do you think he meant about spies in the castle? Who are the spies?"

"Himself, I assume," said Wren wearily. "And this Yannick." She shook her head. "Basil, I'm so sorry. I never dreamed Lex was a threat. He's been working for my family since before I was born."

"You're not to blame," said Basil firmly. He stood, holding out his arms to take Azure from Violet. "Let's get the children to our own rooms. There's not much more to be done until the guards apprehend Yannick, and I think we all need a minute out of the public eye."

"What if Yannick is waiting there?" Wren demanded. "Lex got past the guards—what if this other man did, too?"

"All right, we'll go back to the dining hall," Basil said. "We'll wait there until the guards confirm Yannick has been apprehended."

Wren agreed readily, and the little family made their way into the castle, flanked by a dozen guards. Violet bit her lip as she watched them go, still not satisfied. How had Lex known about that tunnel? Even Basil hadn't remembered it. Was it possible that Lex's perfidy related to Ari's disappearance as well? The old servant had claimed he'd never hurt a Mistran royal, but how much weight could be given to the word of a man who would abduct and terrify a three-year-old child? She didn't have any answers for anything to do with Ari, but the timing was suspicious, to say the least. Where was the Mistran prince? It was impossible that he could have had a hand in the scheme, but had he perhaps discovered it, tried to intervene?

She didn't like to follow that train of thought.

Pushing aside her fears for Ari, Violet's mind circled back to Lex's words about spies *roaming the castle* at will. That claim troubled her. She couldn't shake a suspicion that the servant had meant more than himself and the apparent mastermind, Yannick.

Violet's eyes passed to the pond which dominated the garden, and she drew in a breath. It was absurd to even think it, but...she distinctly remembered kneeling by that pond, trying to convince a lost frog that it wanted to live in this garden. She was sure she'd specifically mentioned the secret tunnel as one of the garden's attractions. But surely the frog couldn't have understood her, let alone passed it on.

Uncertainty trickled over her as she thought about her bizarre pet. It had often seemed to be more than just an average pond frog. And the timing of its appearance in her life was suspicious in light of subsequent events. She'd assumed the frog came from this garden, but in fact, she'd found it in the castle.

And she'd carried it into the royal dining hall time and time again. The frog had always seemed too intelligent, even giving signs of understanding her at times, like with the salt cellar. It had even left her to follow Yannick around more than once.

Suddenly she remembered what the dragons had said the day before—they'd called the frog offensive. She'd thought they were commenting on the unladylike nature of having an amphibian pet, like her mother had done. But since when had dragons cared about human concepts of propriety? Had she misread their meaning completely?

Violet was already running, her mind full of the image from earlier of the dragons flying low over the ocean. Were they still at the shore? She raced through the castle, her lungs burning by the time she threw herself down the cliff path.

There they were!

"Reka, Dannsair," she gasped, forgetting to be sufficiently polite in her haste. "Why did my frog offend you?"

Dannsair blinked slowly at her, and Rekavidur lifted his head from the water, where he was bobbing like an oversized duck.

"Good morning, Princess Violet," Dannsair said in the unhurried way of her kind. "You appear to be distressed."

"Good morning," Violet said impatiently, bobbing her head. "I am distressed. Please, it's important. Why did you say my frog offended you?"

"Because it was true," Rekavidur said, as though the answer was absurdly obvious. "We are not in the habit of speaking untruths. The information being true, and me seeing no reason not to communicate it, I spoke it aloud, aware that it was a matter of some relevance to you."

The dragon actually sounded proud of himself. It was as though he expected Violet to compliment him on his consideration and grasp of human ways because he'd decided to communicate instead of being mysterious and aloof.

"No," said Violet, bursting with impatience. "I didn't mean why did you say it, I meant why was it true? Why did the frog offend you?"

"If that's what you meant, why is that not what you said?" complained Dannsair. "Is accurate communication really so complex?"

Violet could have screamed aloud, but fortunately Rekavidur took pity on her. "I found the creature's presence offensive because of the painful clash of magic that surrounded it. It felt both unnatural and ungainly. It seared my senses."

Dannsair nodded sagely. "In crude terms, it was clumsy and ugly."

Violet stared at them in horror. "If my frog was leaking some kind of twisted magic, why didn't you tell me?"

Rekavidur's expression was haughty as he looked her over. "We told you the creature was offensive. You were not receptive to our communication, and yet you expected us to grace you with more?"

Violet groaned. He wasn't completely wrong, and it was immaterial anyway. She couldn't change the past. Horrible as it was to acknowledge it, the most likely answer to it all seemed to be that her so-called pet carried magic that turned it into a walking, talking—no, hopping, ribbiting—source of surveillance. And she, like a pathetic and lonely fool, had needlessly befriended a frog, handing who knew how much information straight to her family's enemies.

Worst of all, the frog was still roaming free at that moment, somewhere in the castle. And no one would hinder its progress, because it was known to be under her protection. Violet turned to the cliff path, hiking her skirts so she could run. There was no time to lose.

# CHAPTER TWELVE

## *Ari*

Ari hopped along after Yannick with determination. He wasn't going to be deterred or distracted this time. He wanted to see where the young merchant was going. He hung back far enough not to be noticed, his thoughts becoming grim as Yannick traversed the passages with far more confidence than he had a right to.

When his quarry left the building for the eastern courtyard, Ari followed, squeezing through the door before it closed. What was Yannick up to?

He didn't have to wait long to find out. The other man strolled casually across the courtyard, disappearing around a corner of the building. Ari hopped around the corner as well, only just pulling up in time when he realized that Yannick had stopped just out of sight of the main courtyard. And he wasn't alone.

A young woman waited for him, her face lighting with transparent adoration as soon as the merchant appeared. She was a servant at the castle, and Ari had seen her before. In Violet's rooms, that very morning. Naomi, Violet had called her.

Was Yannick involved with her? Was that why he'd wanted to come and stay in the castle? Maybe Ari had misread the nature of Yannick's interest in being near the royals.

In the small space they were occupying, it wasn't so easy for Ari to approach without being seen. Also, he didn't want Naomi to recognize him as the frog from Violet's rooms and get suspicious. Or just squish him. He retreated back past the corner, peering around as best he could without exposing his whole body.

As he watched, the girl stepped forward, sliding her arms around Yannick's neck. The merchant responded in kind, his hands going to her waist, but to Ari's eye his movement wasn't nearly as enthusiastic as hers. Clearly they were involved in a dalliance, but he had a feeling the interest wasn't even on both sides. So why did Yannick allow her to throw herself at him like that? He must have a reason.

The girl began to speak, her tone excited but her words indistinguishable. Ari hesitated, not sure whether he dared to approach closer. She spoke at some length, Yannick responding with a grunt every now and then.

When he spoke, his voice was low and confident, and she listened as rapt as if he were the king himself. Curious as he was about this clandestine rendezvous, Ari began to get restless. There wasn't much point observing them if he couldn't hear what they were saying. Just as he was thinking about edging around the corner, the girl leaned up hopefully, and Yannick rewarded her with a kiss. Again, Ari thought he was a little half-hearted, but she seemed satisfied with the gesture. When the merchant released her, she gave him a glowing smile before starting to walk away, apparently in a daze.

"Remember exactly what we spoke about," Yannick called after her, his voice still low, but now loud enough for Ari to hear. "By now we should be halfway there. If you do your part, we'll be all the way there."

Naomi nodded, her expression determined. Then she slipped away, thankfully not noticing the frog watching her with avid interest.

Yannick emerged in a leisurely way, strolling across the courtyard with an impressive level of unconcern. He was good at behaving naturally, Ari had to give him that. He'd barely gone three strides, however, when a cry went up from one of the guards at the entrance to the building.

"There he is!"

Ari's bulging eyes flicked quickly to the guard in question. He was speaking to another guard, one who seemed to have appeared from inside the castle. A glance at Yannick showed that he'd frozen, his expression still calm but his posture tense.

"He's the one, seize him."

Yannick took a step backward, but he had the presence of mind to realize that trying to escape would seal his fate.

"What's the meaning of this?" he protested, as two guards hurried forward and seized his arms. "I'm sure there's some mistake here. I'm in the castle as the personal guest of Her Highness Princess Violet."

Unable to help himself, Ari let out a deep and disapproving croak at this invocation of Violet's name. It was loud enough to cause one of the guards to glance down at him. A look of confusion crossed the man's face at the sight of a frog loitering in the courtyard, far from any garden, but naturally he didn't pause to investigate the phenomenon.

"You're under arrest on suspicion of orchestrating the kidnapping of Prince Teddy," said the other guard gruffly.

*What?* Horror washed over Ari. Teddy! What had happened to his nephew? Why would Yannick wish the child harm?

"The prince has been kidnapped?" Yannick gasped, his shock annoyingly convincing. But Ari wasn't deceived. The merchant's clandestine meeting with the maid had clearly been one with purpose, not just a lovers' rendezvous.

The maid! She'd left to carry out Yannick's instructions. Could she lead the way to wherever Teddy was being held? Or do some worse mischief if left unsupervised? No one but Ari knew she'd been meeting with Yannick, so even if he'd been caught, she might not come under suspicion until it was too late.

Ari let out a warning ribbit, but all it achieved was to gain more strange looks from the men now hauling Yannick away. From what Ari heard, they were taking him to the dungeons.

Abandoning the group, Ari leaped into motion, hopping frantically toward the castle. He wasn't the fastest of creatures in his current form, but if he pushed himself, using those powerful back legs to their full extent, he could certainly catch up to a walking human. And Naomi wouldn't be running through the castle. That would draw unwanted attention.

Hoping against hope that he wasn't too late to catch her trail, Ari threw himself along the corridor. He wasn't being stealthy this time, and a pair of servants let out a shriek as he squelched past them. Ari didn't care. All that mattered was the form of the maid, just disappearing around a corner up ahead.

He put on some extra speed, his body already exhausted from the unaccustomed exercise. He supposed frogs were quite sedentary creatures, usually. Not this time, he told his amphibian form sternly, refusing to slow his pace.

Naomi made her way to some kind of servants' hall, where Ari was hard pressed to evade notice. He hopped into the room after her, but was forced to dive behind a row of garden boots in order to avoid being stepped on by a pair of serving men bustling past. Peering out from behind the boots, he saw Naomi approach some other maids. She seemed to be asking them a question, her attempt at airy nonchalance not nearly as effective as Yannick's had been. Her expression changed at the others' response, plastering on a look of astonishment that Ari again found unconvincing. She must be hearing the news of Teddy's abduction. In fact, when he took a moment to consider the room around him, Ari realized that the servants were buzzing with the excitement of fresh gossip. Whatever was going on, word had spread.

If Ari was reading Naomi correctly, however, the news was no surprise to her. Which meant she was neck-deep in Yannick's schemes, and it was more important than ever that he keep an eye on her.

He was just contemplating sneaking closer when she turned away from the group, walking a little too quickly as she headed toward a door on the far side of the room.

Abandoning caution, Ari leaped out from behind the boots, scrambling to get his long legs folded under him again as he moved across the room in uneven bounds. Fortunately Naomi had already made it out the door when the first squeals arose, and she didn't stick her head back in to see the source of the commotion.

A middle-aged man in the uniform of a chef's assistant advanced on Ari with purpose, a large bowl in his hand. But Ari sprang to the side, avoiding the man's attempt to trap him and landing splayed on his gangly limbs on top of a table at which several servants were eating.

They all screamed as if he was rabid, seizing their plates and snatching them away. One tried to bash him with a salt cellar, but again Ari was too nimble. His heart was in his throat as he navigated the perils around him, the unassuming humans ten times as terrifying as they should be because they all looked so huge. The room was a melee of noise and movement, and his human mind was barely able to keep his frog instincts—which wanted to give in to blind panic—in check.

Still, there was something exhilarating about the challenge. And he had a feeling this scene would be hilarious to recount if he ever managed to regain his human form. But first, he needed to catch up to Naomi, and stop her from doing anything nefarious.

In spite of the concerted efforts of several humans, Ari made it across the room, darting through the open door and taking off down the corridor in the direction he'd seen Naomi turn. At the first adjoining corridor he flicked his squat little head left and right, catching sight of his quarry just as she approached a large door flanked by guards.

The royal dining hall! Ari scrambled after her, watching in alarm as the guards let her straight through. Why wouldn't they? She was a trusted castle servant, allowed to tend even to the personal suites of the royal family.

Ari pattered after her, his poor little frog body overwhelmed from so much exertion. But he couldn't stop now. He was closing the gap between him and Naomi—he was almost there. With a final leap, he soared through the air just behind the maid.

With a thud followed by a squelch, the guards pulled the door shut, causing Ari to fly straight into it. Dazed, he slid down the wood, landing on the ground with a painful thump.

"What in the…is that a frog?" one of the guards said, his voice tense. Obviously they were all on edge after whatever had happened.

"Do you think it's Princess Violet's pet?" the other said doubtfully. "Do we let it in?"

"Best not to take any risks," said the first one. "I'll catch it and send it outside with the next servant to pass."

Ari's head was still spinning, but those words brought him jolting back into action. He scrambled into a crouch, his eyes assessing the slightly splintered gap at the bottom of the double doors, at the point where the two doors met. It would be tight, but this was no time to be timid.

Throwing himself forward with force, Ari squashed his head into the gap. He heard the guards' startled cries, but he kept going, his long back legs straining as he tried to force himself through. The splinters scratched at his back, but he felt himself moving. Then, all at once, he emerged on the other side with a squelching *pop*.

Unsurprisingly, no one inside the room noticed the small frog suddenly appear at foot level. Even though, as it turned out, there were a lot of people in the room. Ari had often thought the dining hall full when the whole royal family was gathered there, but it was nothing to how the space looked now. All the royals seemed to be present—with the glaring exception of Violet, whose absence Ari noticed straight away—but they were far from the only ones there. Servants and guards were milling around everywhere, watching as the family fussed over a small figure seated on his mother's lap.

Teddy. Ari drooped in relief, some of the tension leaving his miniature frame. Teddy was safe. Whatever scheme Yannick had conceived, it had been thwarted somehow.

Ari was scanning the crowd for Naomi when he saw Obsidian, the husband of Violet's eldest sister, look suddenly around. He and his wife must have been called after Teddy went missing, and gathered with the family. Obsidian's expression was confused, and he was scanning the room as carefully as Ari was. Ari's eyes were just sliding past when the other man's gaze found him, and he stiffened.

Ari swallowed, his whole throat moving convulsively as he

took in Obsidian's expression. Did he have a hatred of frogs or something? Would he squish Ari?

All at once Ari's overwrought mind caught up, and he swelled with excitement. Obsidian was an enchanter! Ari had been wanting to catch him for days. He must have recognized the magic on Ari, just as Ari had hoped he would. Would he be able to help him lift the enchantment?

Before either Ari or Obsidian could make a move, the door banged open, requiring Ari to leap out of the way to avoid being struck. The final member of the family had arrived, and she looked as frantic as Ari had felt a moment before.

"My frog!" Violet called into the packed room. At first Ari thought she'd spotted him, and he crouched, ready to hop to her, but she wasn't finished. "Has anyone seen the frog I've been carrying around? I have to find it *now*!"

The room had gone silent at her abrupt entrance, and everyone was now staring at her blankly.

"Violet?" Zinnia asked. "Is everything all right?"

"No, it's not," said Violet, still sounding panicked. "It's not a normal frog. It's affected by magic, and I've been letting it roam everywhere, spying on us!"

"The frog is there." Obsidian's calm voice cut through her prattle, and everyone followed his pointing finger to see Ari crouched nervously on the floor near Violet's feet. "I'd just located him when you arrived," added Obsidian. "You're right about the magic. It's the strangest and most chaotic signature of power I've ever felt. It drew my attention at once."

"You!" Violet stooped suddenly, seizing Ari and lifting him up before her eyes. "I trusted you—I let you sleep in my rooms! And all along you were some kind of spy working against my own family." She sounded choked with emotion, and Ari could do nothing but swallow in another uncontrollably exaggerated movement.

Without warning, Violet threw him. She was clearly still in the grip of her anger and embarrassment, but even so, Ari could tell she hadn't put her full strength into it. He could only be grateful. After a dizzying moment of the world spinning drunkenly, he hit the stone wall with a painful whump. For the second time in a few minutes, he found himself sliding to the floor, his mind hazy and disoriented.

"Violet!" said someone reproachfully. "Even if you're right, and someone has put magic on the frog, the poor creature likely can't help it. It's not as though it understands."

"You're probably right," said Violet, but she still sounded upset.

Another voice cut across Violet's, raised in a cry that Ari had heard before.

"Tiss! Tiss!" Azure's demand culminated in a wail, and Ari looked up dazedly to see Wren wrestling the buckle of her own belt out of the toddler's grip.

"No, Azure, don't put that in your mouth," said Wren in exasperation. "Stop trying to kiss everything."

Ari froze, his body seeming to grasp the significance of what he'd heard before his mind could catch up. "Tiss" was Zuzu's word for kiss? How many times had he heard his niece say it, and still not grasped what she meant?

Slowly, painfully, an idea trickled into his bruised and addled mind. Azure liked to kiss things. Everything she could get her hands on, in fact. When the students on the hilltop had talked about Entolia's princesses, he'd thought only of King Basil's twelve sisters. Well, if he was honest, he'd thought only of one of those twelve sisters. But Violet wasn't going to kiss a frog for no apparent reason—he'd never really considered that an option for getting out of the curse.

Somehow, he'd forgotten all about King Basil's daughter. But she was every bit as much a princess as her aunts.

These thoughts were still coming together in Ari's mind when Wren's soft voice once again reached his ears.

"Yes, thank you, if you could take her for a moment," the queen said to someone, sounding relieved to relinquish the still-protesting toddler.

Ari looked up, horror racing over him as he recognized the maid who was so helpfully offering to hold the child for a moment. Naomi.

Obsidian, who'd crossed the room to speak to Violet, turned to Ari, leaning down as if to pick him up and examine him more closely. Giving himself no more time to think, Ari leaped back into motion, propelling himself off the floor toward Naomi. A few others grabbed at him, but he'd become adept at dodging, and he evaded them with ease. The maid was backing away, hugging the child to her as if to protect Azure.

Ari ignored her, pausing at her feet to gather himself, then springing up in a huge hop, aiming straight for Azure. He landed on the toddler's chubby arm, clinging on for dear life. With a squeal of delight, his niece stopped crying at once, seizing the frog in one surprisingly strong fist.

Cries of alarm rang out from all sides, more than one person screaming for Azure to stop. Naomi just seemed stunned, frozen in place with apparently no idea what to do. Azure, on the other hand, just squealed more loudly as she lifted Ari, squeezing so tightly it was all he could do to draw breath. His frog instincts were desperately telling him to slip free, but he held them at bay, his protuberant eyes fixed hopefully on Azure.

"Tiss!" the child cried gleefully.

"No, Zuzu, don't put that thing in your—"

Wren's alarmed words were cut off as Azure mashed Ari to her mouth in a clumsy motion.

*BOOM.*

With a shattering crash that Ari had never witnessed with

the magic of an accomplished enchanter, he fell to the floor, his form writhing and twisting and stretching. It was a terrifying, disconcerting experience, but after a few chaotic moments, Ari found himself lying on the stone, whole and unharmed and mercifully human.

# CHAPTER THIRTEEN

## Ari

The screams and cries that rang out put everyone's previous protests to shame. Ari's eyes flicked for the briefest moment to Violet, noting that her face showed nothing but blank, total shock. Then he remembered the task at hand, and he spun back around to face Naomi, who was still clutching Azure.

Ari was still wearing exactly what he had been when he'd fallen afoul of the students' clumsy enchantment, and unfortunately he hadn't been wearing a sword on that occasion. But a guard had approached, white-faced with shock, to assist the missing prince to his feet. Ari disregarded his offer, instead seizing the man's sword and drawing it, turning to the traitorous maid in the same fluid motion.

"Put my niece down," he growled. "Now."

"I…but…Your Highness, I…" Naomi stuttered, her wide eyes fixed on the tip of Ari's blade.

"I know you're in league with Yannick," he said calmly. "I saw you with him, and I heard him give you instructions. If you think I'm going to allow you to steal Princess Azure, you've lost your mind."

Open fear was on Naomi's face now, and her eyes flew frantically to each of the room's exits. Guards stepped up on either side of Ari, their faces hard and menacing as they drew weapons of their own.

All at once, Naomi gave up. With a sob, she curled in on herself, dropping Azure like she was suddenly burning hot to the touch.

Ari dropped his pilfered sword, diving forward to catch the child before she hit the floor. It took all his focus to reach out his arms to intercept her—his poor, addled mind was trying to tell him to catch her with a flick of the tongue.

A shudder went over him, and he determined to take the details of his fly-eating moments to the grave. The sound of running feet reached him, and he turned to see Wren and Basil both hurrying forward. The looks on their faces cut him to the heart. He handed Azure over mutely, watching as the guards seized Naomi from either side.

"Ari." Violet's whisper instantly claimed Ari's attention. He whipped around to see her moving toward him, almost like she was in a trance. Her eyes were fixed on his, and her face was pale. "You were the frog? The frog was you...the whole time?"

Ari nodded slowly. He could almost see her mind whirring, going back over all her interactions with her pet amphibian. Hopefully she'd remember that he'd respected her privacy. A pained look passed over Violet's face, and Ari held his breath.

"I'm sorry I shoved you in my pocket," she said. "And called you slimy, if I recall."

A laugh burst out of Ari, the sound unsteady. He passed a hand through his hair, reveling in the return of his familiar human form. "Actually, you said I wasn't slimy," he reassured her. "I think you complimented me on my cleanliness."

Someone groaned, but a slow grin was spreading across Violet's face.

"That's right," she recalled. "I think what I actually said was that you weren't as slimy as I expected. You were definitely still slimy."

"My apologies," said Ari solemnly, and Violet's grin became a chuckle.

"Ari, this is too ridiculous," said Wren, sounding impatient more than anything. "First a swan, then this? How in dragon's flame did you get yourself turned into a *frog*?"

He shrugged. "I just felt like a change. Too long as a human, you know."

"Ari." His sister's usually gentle voice was almost a growl.

Ari raised his hands in surrender, laughing. "All right, I'll explain. But it's a bit of a pitiful story to be perfectly honest. I wasn't even part of some sinister plot. It was all a stupid accident."

He proceeded to explain what had happened the night he'd turned into a frog, sprinkling the tale with humorous details in hopes of getting another laugh out of Violet. It always felt like a victory, getting her to laugh. And after all, he'd much rather his story be entertaining than tragic. Now that he was restored to his human form—and after only a matter of days rather than years—he was inclined to focus on the comical absurdity of it all.

Obsidian groaned aloud when Ari got to the part about the cocky magic student.

"I'll have his hide," muttered the enchanter to no one in particular.

Ari chuckled, unsurprised to learn that the student in question was known to those in charge.

"So how did you break it?" asked Briar, Violet's sixteen-year-old sister.

"Oh, I forgot to explain the counterforce," said Ari. "The

students went for something they called traditional—a kiss from a princess."

Obsidian groaned again. "Foolish old superstitions," he said. "Why is everyone so convinced that kisses have some kind of potent magical properties? They're entirely ordinary."

"As your wife, I take offense at that," interjected Zinnia.

The look her husband gave her somehow managed to be both fond and exasperated. "You know what I mean."

"Anyway, I didn't think I could convince Vi—any of you girls to kiss me in my frog form," Ari said, hastily trying to cover his slip. The smirks from various of his listeners told him he'd failed. Violet wasn't smirking, though. Her cheeks had gone delightfully pink. "I thought I'd have to find another way around it, until just now when Azure was trying to kiss anything and everything, and I realized she's a princess too…"

He trailed off, sending a wink to his niece. "Thanks for saving me, Zuzu. Don't ever change."

Wren let out a soft sigh, and Ari winked at her as well. No doubt she wouldn't mind her daughter changing that one habit in particular.

"We were all so confused and worried when you went missing," Violet said, recapturing his attention. Her gaze was full of meaning as it rested on his face. "*I* was so confused."

Ari turned fully to face her, stepping forward and taking her hand in his. "I'm sorry about that night," he said. "It was unlike me. I didn't understand it myself at the time. But once I got outside the castle, I realized I was following some kind of magical compulsion."

"You were?" Violet's eyes were wide. "I think…I think I knew that," she said slowly. "Or at least, some part of me suspected it. That explains my dream. But I never realized what it meant."

"Your dream?" Ari repeated, confused.

"Never mind," said Violet. "Go on."

Ari let out a breath. "It was the golden ball. The one that my parents apparently sent as a gift for the children, although I'd never heard about it. It was a talisman."

"The ball?" said Wren sharply. "So it wasn't from our parents at all?" Her face fell. "It must have been Lex who brought it, I suppose."

"Lex?" Ari asked, perplexed.

She raised miserable eyes to his. "He's the one who kidnapped Teddy. He was working with Yannick."

"What?!" Ari stared at her open-mouthed. "Lex? Surely you're wrong." He just couldn't believe it.

"I wish I was," Wren said softly. "But Basil found him holding Teddy captive."

"I've just realized something," Violet interjected. "Lex was hovering nearby when I told you about the secret tunnel in the garden, wasn't he? He must have overheard and gone looking. How could I have forgotten he was there?"

"The secret tunnel?" Ari was lost again, but Violet shook her head impatiently.

"Finish what you were saying about that golden ball."

"Yes, is the ball on you now?" The question came from Obsidian. "There's still magic hanging about your person."

With a frown, Ari felt in his pockets, fishing out the small golden ball. "I guess it was somehow wrapped up in my frog form all this time," he commented. "Like my clothing."

"Thank goodness for that," muttered someone. Lilac, he was fairly sure.

Violet grinned, but the expression faded as she studied the ball. "What's its purpose?"

"I don't exactly know," said Ari. He turned it over in his mind. "It was drawing me somewhere, and the longer I handled it, the stronger the compulsion got. I think I was following someone, but I couldn't get a good look at them.

Then I ended up on the trail of one of those students, and, well, you've heard the rest."

"I don't understand," said one of Violet's sisters, frowning. "How are those students mixed up in this? Were they working with the ones who kidnapped Teddy?"

Ari shook his head. "I really don't think so. It was just a very unlucky accident that I got in the way of that enchantment. They didn't know I'd been hit with the magic—they didn't even know I was there. There's no reason to think they knew about the golden ball. Whoever it was drawing me toward was someone different. I suppose they just chose to walk along the same hilltop."

"Ari," said Violet, her tone strange. "Why are you moving?"

"What?" Ari looked down at her, realizing as he did so that she was right. He'd taken a step to the side without even noticing it. "I don't know," he said. With an effort, he relaxed his mind, and instantly he felt it. The compulsion. He let his feet lead him another step, and then another. Next thing he knew, he was standing in front of the guards who still gripped Naomi. "You," he breathed, lifting the ball and staring from it to her.

Naomi said nothing, but her gasping breaths and terrified face said it all. Yannick had chosen his conspirator poorly. She had nothing like the cool control he did. But then, she was clearly besotted enough to do whatever he asked of her, which had its own value, Ari supposed.

"The ball was drawing me toward you," he said slowly.

"Naomi was there that night," Violet interjected. "She was in the dining hall. I remember seeing her when I glanced in, and noted that you were staring at the row of pretty young serving girls."

Ari gave her a pained look, but didn't chastise her aloud for her lack of faith in him. As if he could have found any of those strangers pretty when he had Violet in front of him. He returned his attention to Naomi.

"I think I understand. The ball was intended to make the children wander in your direction, to make it easier for you to take them without being noticed." He shook his head. "Lex may have carried the ball into the castle, but Yannick is the one who orchestrated the enchantment, isn't he? That's why he needed you. But once the ball went missing—my one useful contribution to this whole disaster—he had to improvise. So he weaseled his way into the castle to oversee the kidnapping himself."

"That's not why he needed me," Naomi burst out unexpectedly, her voice quivering with passion. "He included me in his plans because he loves me. We both love each other."

Ari said nothing, almost able to pity the deluded girl. He'd seen the embrace she and Yannick had shared, and he had no doubt whatsoever that the merchant had been using her for his own purposes.

"Either way, he probably never intended to go through with my offer to marry him," Violet said thoughtfully. "That's a relief, in a way."

"What?!" Ari's and Basil's voices rang out in unison.

Violet shrugged, looking between Ari and her brother. "We had to find a solution to the merchant crisis. I told you it was about ego, Basil. You should have seen how quickly Ulrich changed his tune when I suggested the idea."

"Merchant crisis be hanged!" Basil said curtly. "There's no way I would let you sacrifice yourself like that."

"I suspected you'd take that attitude," Violet commented calmly. "That's why I didn't tell you. But there's no need to get worked up," she added quickly, as Basil opened his mouth to protest further. "Obviously I won't be marrying him now."

"I should think not," Basil said darkly. He turned to Naomi.

"There are a lot of questions still not answered to my satisfaction. I want to know exactly what was planned against my children, and why." He nodded to the guards. "Bring both Lex and Yannick from the dungeons. We'll have this out here and now."

Half a dozen guards trotted off at this command, and the rest of the group waited tensely for their return. Violet came alongside Ari, her presence warm and reassuring.

"I still can't believe you were the frog," she murmured after a few minutes. "You owe me a new pet." Ari chuckled as she studied him thoughtfully. "I'm very glad you weren't yourself when you ran out on me like that," she told him.

Ari's gaze softened, and he slipped his hand into hers to give it a squeeze. "I'd like a second chance at that conversation," he informed her.

"Conversation?" she repeated, her expression provocative. "That's not what I call it."

Ari was prevented from replying as the door opened. The prisoners were led in, chained and surrounded, and their bantering mood fell away at once.

Basil moved forward, his eyes hard as they passed between the three conspirators.

"Speak, one of you," he said, his voice sending a chill over Ari.

"Your Majesty, you are operating under an absurd mistake," Yannick said smoothly. "And I can't help but fear that my father will be gravely offended when he learns of how I have been treated. I have no knowledge of whatever events have led to such a—"

"Don't be a fool, boy." Lex cut this eloquence off brutally. "Your precious plans didn't work, and we've been caught. If you think I'm going to keep my mouth shut to protect you, you're mad. I'll tell them everything you did and said."

A look of fury crossed Yannick's face, but he managed to

keep his voice steady. "You, sir, are mistaken. And you have absolutely no evidence to incriminate me in—"

"Enough," said Basil sharply. "You were seen by Prince Ari discussing the matter with this young woman." He gestured to Naomi. "And we have evidence that the artifact given to my children in the guise of a gift contains magic intended to draw the children to her. I have more knowledge of the black market dealings of non-guild enchanters than you imagine, and I have no doubt that inquiries by my agents will yield all the information I could desire. I'm not interested in excuses." His eyes swung to Lex, perhaps identifying the one most likely to talk. "What I want to know is why."

Lex said nothing, at least until Wren stepped up beside her husband. "Yes, why, Lex?" she asked, tears in her eyes. "How could you betray me and my family like this?"

"Betray your family?" Lex burst out. "I've done nothing of the kind, Your Highness. It's you who've done that, and it breaks my heart to say it."

Wren drew in a breath as Basil let out an angry hiss. Ari knew it wasn't new for them to encounter this reaction to their union and the alliance it represented. But to hear it from Lex, who'd been part of his daily life for as long as he could remember, was more personal, and undeniably more painful.

"Don't misunderstand me," Lex said pleadingly. "I told the truth in the garden—I would never have harmed either of the children, or allowed anyone else to do so. They're part of the Mistran royal family. They belong in their own kingdom, with their own family."

"Basil and I are their family," said Wren passionately. "Your attempts to justify your behavior are the most despicable part of it all."

"And they make no sense," said Basil coldly. "If you weren't going to harm them, why take them?"

"The plan was to hold them hostage to compel you to abdicate on behalf of yourself and your line," said Lex stonily, his eyes on Basil. "Then Princess Wren and her children could return to Mistra, where they belong. The royal lines of our kingdoms should never have been mingled. Mistra and Entolia are enemies, and always will be."

"They always will be in the minds of people like you," Basil corrected, sounding weary now. "People unwilling to let go of the past."

"Hold on." Zinnia seemed to be focused on a different detail. "If Basil abdicated for himself and his children, that would make *me* the monarch."

"Save us all," said Lilac dryly.

"Wren's right, this whole plan is despicable," said Zinnia with feeling. "How dare you, all of you? I don't want to be *queen!*"

In spite of the gravity of the situation, Ari's lips twitched at this evidence of what aspect of the whole debacle offended Zinnia most.

"Obsidian, we'd be the rulers," she said, apparently dissatisfied with her husband's failure to express adequate horror at the idea. "Our whole lives would be *ruined.*"

"Thanks, Zin," said Basil dryly.

"I suspect that may have been part of the point," said Obsidian quietly.

Everyone frowned at him, his wife as confused as the rest of them. "What do you mean?" Zinnia asked.

Obsidian shrugged. "I don't mean to sound arrogant, but I suspect I may have featured in their motivation. It's not the first time I've heard mutters about how beneficial it would be to have an enchanter on the throne. It's nonsense, of course. But people so often value magic much more highly than it deserves."

Zinnia drew in a sharp breath, her eyes flying to Yannick. "He's right, isn't he? You liked the idea of Obsidian ruling by my side. Of all the cheek!" She narrowed her eyes. "The joke would have been on you, because I would have abdicated as well. Lilac would make a better queen than I would."

Ari glanced at the family's second daughter, noting that she looked both surprised and gratified by her sister's praise.

"But you tried to plan for that eventuality, too, didn't you?" Violet said slowly, her eyes on Yannick. "When I suggested a marriage alliance, you basically asked if you could marry Lilac instead. You didn't count on it—you must have known it was a long shot—but you actually hoped *you* could be in the running for ruler, didn't you? You little snake."

"Yannick?" Naomi sounded uncertain for the first time. "You...you didn't plan to marry a princess, did you?"

"Stop making a fool of yourself, Naomi," said Yannick brutally, his calm mask falling away. "Did you truly think I would marry you? A servant girl with nothing but a weak heart and a gullible mind to recommend you?"

Naomi gasped, then began to cry openly. It was a painful sight, and Ari looked away. No doubt the girl had believed Yannick would marry her, and she would one day inherit his father's vast merchant empire with him. Instead, she'd lost everything, and she would likely be thrown into prison.

"How can you claim that Mistra and Entolia can never be anything but enemies, while at the same time plotting with Entolians for a common purpose?" Wren asked Lex, pointedly turning away from the scene between the merchant and the maid. Her heartbreak over Lex's betrayal was still plain on her face. "Can't you see the hypocrisy in that?"

"We briefly had the same end," said Lex stiffly. "That doesn't mean we're allies."

"Yes it does," Basil contradicted. "That's often all allies are."

He frowned. "I don't understand how you made your plans, though. When did you even—ah." He glanced at Yannick. "Your visit to Myst a short time ago, on behalf of the Merchants' Guild. That's when you and Lex connected? You weren't exaggerating when you said it was an informative visit."

"You masked your evil intentions well, Yannick, I'll give you that," said Violet coldly. "But have you no shame? Your father I can understand. He's self-important and overly dramatic, but at least it makes some kind of sense for him to want to see Mistran merchants banned from his most profitable marketplace. It's a response that relates to his grievance. You, though. Were you really so disgruntled over the Mistran merchants moving in on your family's trade that you were willing to abduct the heir to the throne? Was such drastic action as kidnapping two young children really required?"

Yannick made a dismissive noise in his throat. "Drastic action was required. The alliance between Mistra and Entolia is a travesty. The advantages to the Mistran merchants are an example of the alliance's evils, certainly, but they're hardly a central one." His eyes passed to Basil, and he yanked one arm, as if trying to free it from the guard who held it. "You know what you've done. You know how you've insulted your own people with the way you ended the war. My best friend fought and *died* to beat back the Mistrans. And his own king openly dishonored his sacrifice by welcoming the enemy into our kingdom—onto the *throne*—with open arms."

Ari tensed at this insult to his sister and his people. But Wren met Yannick's eyes calmly, with no hint of the emotion she'd shown at Lex's more personal betrayal. Obviously she was inured to this attitude in her new people. Ari's heart ached for her. He hadn't realized it could be this bad.

Ari's eyes passed to Lex, whose face was stony as he listened to Yannick's angry words. The old servant's own motivations weren't so different from the Entolian's. Ari remembered Lex's reaction when they'd crossed the former front lines, and the grizzled servant's explanation that he'd been stationed there for a while during the war. Who knew what he'd seen in that time to create such an unshakable hatred for the Entolians? And even back in the Mistran capital, he'd seen the effect of the war on the royal family he served. It had been a grim time.

"Queen Wren is right." Obsidian re-entered the conversation unexpectedly. Ari had heard him speak more during this confrontation than during the entire rest of his time in Tola. "Whether you wish to acknowledge it or not, you are united by your anger about the alliance between our two kingdoms. Calling our peoples natural enemies while working together in an attempt to prove that we *shouldn't* be allies is the most absurd hypocrisy."

Obsidian shifted forward, his upright—almost rigid—posture reminding Ari that he was a lieutenant as well as an enchanter, and had served in the war himself.

"I fought in the war," he said, his eyes passing from Lex to Yannick. "And I lost someone very dear to me. You're not the only ones who suffered from the conflict. Far from it. But you'd rather pretend no one understands your pain, because it's easier than admitting that there's another way to respond. That you could choose to forgive and move forward. Instead you're choosing anger and violence. The very things we all hated about the war."

His eyes passed to Basil and Wren, standing nearby with their children cocooned between them. As glad as he was to see the family all safe and together, Ari's heart was heavy as he looked at them. It would probably be some time before they would be able to relax again, after watching attempted kidnappings of both their children, in each case perpetrated by someone they trusted.

"You know there's a better way," Obsidian went on, still addressing the conspirators. "You've seen it. You have no excuse."

None of the three had anything to say in response to these words, and at an order from Basil, the guards carted them away. Ari let out a long breath. There would be plenty more headaches to come as the situation was fully dealt with, but for the moment they could all afford to lower their guard. The threat was past. Under the direction of the steward, most of the servants and guards trickled from the room, leaving only the royal family and a few necessary attendants.

"I've just realized something," Violet said thoughtfully from beside Ari. "Naomi does my hair sometimes, and she's been strange ever since you arrived, Ari. She was asking me about you from the start, trying to draw me out into acknowledging a connection between us. No wonder she was concerned. A second marriage of alliance between you and me would be the last thing they would have wanted."

A few of Violet's sisters let out choking laughs, and Ari found himself grinning as well.

"It's good to see that the misadventures of the past few days haven't changed you, Violet," he said in a mock solemn tone. "You're just as eager to propose to me as ever. You Entolians sure know how to make a man feel welcome."

"I...I didn't..." Violet's cheeks reddened, her usual witty banter failing her.

"I'm sorry, I shouldn't tease you," said Ari quickly. He squeezed her hand, sending a quick glance around the room at their large audience. "Can you spare a minute?"

Violet nodded mutely, and Ari tugged her across the room, heading for the very patio where she'd taken him on his first night. This time, he pulled her down the steps and into the small gardens beyond, continuing until a shrub hid them from the window's view.

"Standing behind a plant? How disappointing," Violet said, in an unconvincing attempt at her usual teasing tone. "I thought you would at least scale the building."

Ari chuckled at this reference to their first private conversation. "I would, but I'm concerned that perching on a rooftop would make it harder."

"Make what harder?" Violet asked suspiciously.

Ari didn't answer her. "I said I wanted a second chance at this." He searched her eyes. "Violet, I fell for you the very first night." He jerked his head back toward the building. "The moment you climbed that wall, I think. I have no interest in going across the desert anymore. I haven't for some time. I want..." He drew a deep breath. "I want to stay here, with you. Forever. Only if you'll have me, of course."

Violet's eyes were glowing, and her hands slipped up onto his chest. "I want nothing more, Ari." Her cheeks were pink again. "I don't know exactly when I fell in love with you, but I knew it for sure when I thought you were gone. I couldn't help falling for you—you made me feel so *seen*." Her eyes softened. "And that didn't even change after you disappeared, did it? You saw me and helped me even when you were a *frog*, for goodness' sake. Listening to me at meals when I couldn't get anyone else to hear me...the necklace was you, wasn't it?"

Ari nodded, touching a finger to the silver chain, which he'd only just noticed was suspended around her neck. "I retrieved it with my sticky frog tongue," he informed her candidly. "It was quite disgusting. You probably want to wash it."

Violet laughed, and Ari slipped his hands over hers where they still rested on his chest. Her touch was warm and exhilarating, every nerve of his body extra responsive after his time in a different—and much less appealing—form.

"Of course I saw you, Violet," he said softly. "How could I not? From the first time I looked at you, I couldn't take my eyes off you. You're...incomparable. There's no one in the world like you."

There was plenty more he could say about her, but he wasn't given the chance. Violet pushed up on her toes, and Ari dipped his head in response, his thoughts and instincts delightfully in sync.

Their lips met at last, the embrace all the sweeter for the interruption that had been forced on this moment. Ari's hands slipped around Violet's waist, pulling her against him as he kissed her passionately. Her hands fisted in his tunic, her lips moving eagerly against his. Ari never wanted the moment to end, but far too soon, Violet pulled back, apparently to catch her breath.

He supposed breathing was a valid excuse for not doing that every minute of every day. But just barely.

"Don't you think that would have been harder if we were perched on a roof?" he asked, grinning contentedly at her.

Violet chuckled. "Definitely. I'm pretty sure I would have plummeted off the edge, given how my head was just spinning."

Ari smiled at the compliment to his kissing skills, but her lighthearted words triggered a darker thought in his mind. "It seems you were close to plummeting off a different kind of edge while I was gone," he said quietly. "Were you really planning to marry that merchant, Yannick, without even telling me?"

Violet's expression became serious at once. She reached up a hand to Ari's cheek, her soft touch a greater balm than any apology.

"I formulated that plan long before you arrived," she told

him. "And I was seriously second-guessing whether I could go through with it by the time you disappeared. But then you just walked out on me—or so I thought—and I admit, I threw myself into my cold-blooded plan all the more determinedly because of it. I didn't want to acknowledge to myself that I had a broken heart. It was easier to pretend I didn't have much of a heart, and there was no reason not to form a political alliance."

Ari nodded, not liking the whole situation, but recognizing that there was nothing to be gained by distressing himself over what-ifs. Yannick was very much out of the picture, and Violet would never be called upon to sacrifice her heart in that way.

"All right lovebirds, wherever you are." Wren's voice issued from the room now concealed behind the shrub. "There's more to discuss in here."

Ari grimaced at Violet. "Sisters."

"You don't know the half of it," Violet laughed back at him. "Only one sister, and as sweet as Wren? You have no right to complain."

Ari laughed as well, twining his fingers through hers and leading the way back through the gardens. They'd barely entered the room when Briar challenged them, her eyes flying from their clasped hands to their faces.

"So that's it, then? You're going to get married now?"

"That's the plan," said Violet cheerfully. "Ari wants to stay in Tola, and I said it would be fine, I guess."

"Something tells me that's not what you said," Zinnia interjected, grinning.

"Oh, Ari, it would be so wonderful to have you living here!" Wren said, her face shining. "I hoped it when I saw how you two hit it off, but I didn't want to push in case I scared you away. You seemed so excited about the idea of crossing the desert."

Ari shook his head. "I was excited. And yet, it's amazing

how quickly any interest in that idea faded away once I started spending time with Violet. I think the truth is I was desperate for a change, and anything new would have felt like an adventure." He grinned at his sister. "At least this is a change our parents will have to approve of, since it brings political benefit."

"Not much," said Briar, with the frankness Ari was already coming to expect from her. "We already have an alliance through Basil and Wren. You two marrying won't change much." Her tone was unemotional as she addressed her next words to her sister. "At least marrying Yannick would have resolved an active problem, Violet."

"We'll have no more talk of that," said Basil, speaking with a sternness Ari had rarely heard him direct toward his sisters. "Violet, I know you meant well, but it was a horrible plan."

His gaze flicked to his wife, softening slightly. "Marriage isn't a quick solution to any problem, no matter how dire. It's a serious business, and it's lifelong. I'd far rather the embargo go ahead than sacrifice the future happiness of any of my sisters to stop it. Besides," his voice turned dry, "there will certainly be no embargo. Ulrich may not have had a hand in his son's treasonous plans, but they've still removed any bargaining power he had. I doubt the rest of the guild will continue to blindly follow his lead when word gets out that his son is in the dungeons. If he wants me to show mercy and refrain from seeing Yannick hang for trying to abduct my children, he'll fall in line very quickly."

Ari regarded his usually even-tempered brother-in-law with new respect. He hadn't often appreciated what it must cost to take on the role of monarch so young. Basil wore it remarkably well.

"Well, I'm sure it's all very nice that everyone's marriages are working out," said Briar impatiently. "But some of us have much more interesting questions we want answers to."

"Agreed." Wisteria, the youngest, stepped forward to join her older sister. "Tell us everything, Ari. What was it like?"

"Did you eat flies?" nine-year-old Ivy demanded. "Did you catch things with your tongue?"

"We know you ribbited," said Wisteria solemnly. "We *heard* you."

"Uh..." Ari dithered, unsure where to start.

Violet was openly laughing by now, her eyes dancing as they met his. "First a swan, then a frog...I think you really must be the unluckiest prince in all Solstice," she informed him.

Ari shook his head, a smile playing on his lips as he put an arm around her shoulder and drew her close.

"Actually," he told her, "I'm completely convinced that I'm the luckiest."

He was sure he heard one of the younger girls groan, but he didn't care about the audience. He only cared about the pink tint to Violet's cheeks, and the smile she wasn't quite able to hide. She was pleased, and that was all that mattered.

He lowered his head, pressing a kiss to her forehead as she leaned against him. With any luck, he would spend the rest of his life making her as happy as he felt in this moment. Hopefully in human form. Because, he reflected, as Violet slipped her arm around his waist in a comfortably familiar gesture, there was a lot to be said for arms that could hold and lips that could kiss.

After all, what princess in her right mind would want to kiss a frog?

# NEXT IN ONCE UPON A PRINCE

Available October 6th 2023

**An unwilling suitor. A mocking princess. A marriage they both abhor.**

Diplomacy and a demanding mother send Thorben of Hauke to a neighboring kingdom, there to present himself as candidate for marriage to their princess. Beautiful Leonie of Elisia is famous for insulting every suitor she receives, and Thorben banks on her dismissing him as well—which she does, with vicious aplomb.

This time, though, her ridicule proves her father's breaking point. The King of Elisia vows that Leonie will marry a beggar, and Thorben departs inwardly applauding the punishment... until a terrible storm deposits him tattered and bedraggled at the castle's kitchen door. Before he can weasel out of his mishap—or even pull rank—the marriage is done.

But what's legal in Elisia might not be in Hauke. Disguised as a beggar, Thorben leads Leonie home to secure an annulment.

If he's lucky, he'll get it without revealing his true identity... and before losing his heart to his exquisite but sharp-tongued bride.

**The Beggar Prince, a retelling of King Thrushbeard, is book 2 of Once Upon A Prince, a multi-author series of clean fairy tale retellings. Each standalone story features a swoony prince fighting for his happily ever after.**

# Once Upon A Prince

The Unlucky Prince by Deborah Grace White
The Beggar Prince by Kate Stradling
The Golden Prince by Alice Ivinya
The Wicked Prince by Celeste Baxendell
The Midnight Prince by Angie Grigaliunas
The Poisoned Prince by Kristin J. Dawson
The Silver Prince by Lyndsey Hall
The Shoeless Prince by Jacque Stevens
The Silent Prince by C. J. Brightley
The Crownless Prince by Selina R. Gonzalez
The Awakened Prince by Alora Carter
The Winter Prince by Constance Lopez
***Grab the whole Once Upon A Prince series today!***

# NOTE FROM THE AUTHOR

Thank you for reading *The Unlucky Prince*. I hope you enjoyed visiting the world of Solstice. I would be so grateful if you would consider leaving a review on Amazon—it would really make a difference!

Are you yet to discover *The Kingdom Tales*, the series set immediately before *The Unlucky Prince*? These six interconnected standalone fairy tale retellings will sweep you away to a world where dragons do their own thing, enchanters run amok, and happily ever afters require some chasing. If you enjoy strong heroines, clean romance, and fantasy worlds with a dash of intrigue, then lose yourself in the fairy tale world of *The Kingdom Tales* today.

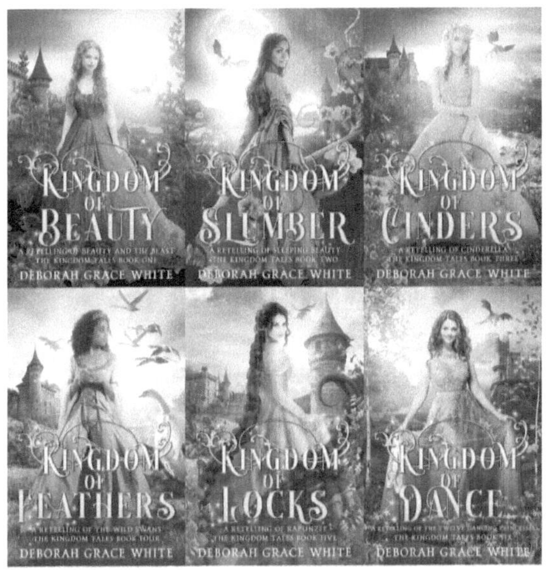

Join up to my mailing list at deborahgracewhite.com to be kept up to date on new releases, specials, and giveaways, such as bonus chapters. You'll receive some great freebies, too, including *An Expectation of Magic*, a novella which is a prequel to my completed YA fantasy series *The Vazula Chronicles*.

Plus, you'll receive *Dragon's Sight*, an 8,000 word prequel to my completed YA fantasy trilogy *The Kyona Chronicles*.

Again, thanks for entering the world of Solstice! I hope to see you back again.

# ALSO BY DEBORAH GRACE WHITE

The Kyona Chronicles: YA Fantasy

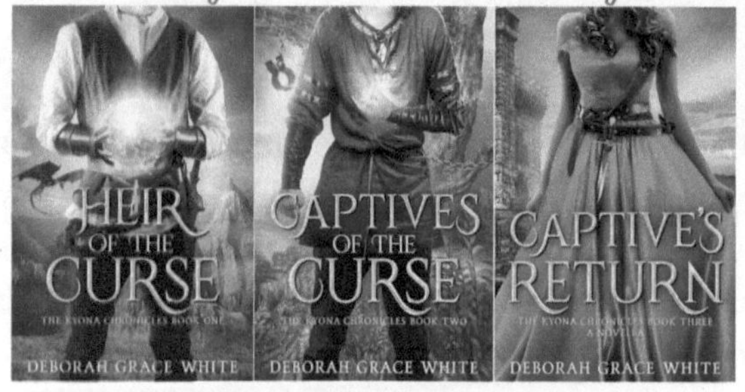

The Kyona Legacy: YA Fantasy

## The Vazula Chronicles: YA Fantasy

## The Kingdom Tales: Fairy Tale Retellings

## The Singer Tales: Fairy Tale Retellings
## (releasing throughout 2023)

## The Unlucky Prince: Fairy Tale Retelling
## (Once Upon a Prince Multi-Author Series)

# Acknowledgments

As always, I'm so grateful to my wonderfully supportive team for helping to make *The Unlucky Prince* happen.

Ray, my incredible husband, for being the first to hear the story, and helping make it better. My betas for their great feedback: Alora, Constance, Mel W, Mum, Adrian, and Dad. Thanks also to Shae for the excellent job proofreading. Any remaining errors are of course my own.

Thanks to MoorBooks for the stunning cover that so perfectly captures both Ari and Violet, and to Becca for the gorgeous map that continues to bring Solstice to life.

To you, the reader, thank you for giving me the privilege of being an author.

And most importantly, to God, who truly sees us, no matter how small we feel.

# About the Author

I've been a reader since I can remember, growing up on a wide range of books, from classic literature to light-hearted romps. The love of reading has traveled with me unchanged across multiple continents, and carried me from my own childhood all the way to having children of my own.

But if reading is like looking through a window into a magical and beautiful world, beginning to write my own stories was like discovering that I could open that window and climb right out into fantasyland.

I cannot believe how privileged I am to actually be living that childhood dream and publishing my own novels. I do so from my hometown of Adelaide, Australia, where I live with my husband and our three little ones.

I've never outgrown my love of young adult stories, so the genre of young adult fantasy was always going to be my niche. Feel free to email me at deborah@deborahgracewhite.com and introduce yourself! Or subscribe to my mailing list at deborah gracewhite.com for free giveaways, sales, and updates.